Wives and Lovers

'Please, Jack! Don't deny it. It's no good. I *know*, Jack. Can't you see? I know there is another woman and I know who she is. And, as from now, you are not sharing my bed any more. You'll have to use the box room or Grandad's room from now on, not our room or our bed. And I want to know what you intend doing about me. Shall I leave after the holiday? Find another house? Tell me what you want me to do, Jack . . .'

All Pat's anger and anxiety poured out, and having released her fears in this confrontation with Jack, she burst into tears and ran from the kitchen. Jack sat stunned, his scone half eaten and his own mind now in a turmoil. He went upstairs to his room and sat with his head in his hands, his eyes moist with unshed tears and his heart full of the sorrow he had caused. And he knew that he could not leave Pat, the farm, this kind of life.

But he could not leave Karen either.

JAMES FERGUSON

Wives and Lovers
Emmerdale Farm Book 24

Based on the successful
Yorkshire Television series
originated by Kevin Laffan

FONTANA/Collins

First published in Great Britain by
Fontana Paperbacks 1989

Copyright © 1989 James Ferguson

Front cover photograph courtesy Yorkshire Television
Stills Department
© Yorkshire Television Ltd 1988
Emmerdale and Emmerdale Farm are Trade Marks of
Yorkshire Television Ltd

Chapter One

Annie Sugden glanced at the clock on the kitchen wall of Emmerdale Farm. 'It's half past eight!' she cried. 'And Dad's not up yet. I'd best give him a call.'

Pat smiled. 'It's all that celebrating, Ma. He had a good night at the Woolpack, remember, letting all Beckindale know he'd beaten Seth and the rest with their pumpkins. He did have a few glasses of cider; mebbe it was more than just a few! But he did enjoy himself. He'll be sleeping it off now.'

Annie smiled at the recollection of Sam Pearson returning from the Woolpack last night; he had been overjoyed at his little success and there was no doubt that the celebrations with both friends and competitors had been uproarious. As he had come home afterwards there had been just a hint of uncertainty in his walk, and he'd stumbled over the threshold, giggling like a child.

'It does him good to get among his pals once in a while, and let his hair down,' she agreed. 'And you know what he's like when it comes to gardening – he always wants to grow the biggest and best of everything, whether it's cabbages, carrots – or pumpkins! But he's never been one for sleeping in, not even after a night like last night. I'll take him a cup of tea – just to remind him that morning has come!'

'And I'll get his breakfast ready,' offered Pat.

As Annie climbed the stairs with a cup of tea in her hand, Pat could not help noticing that her mother-in-law was finding it hard work; she had the movements of a woman who was beginning to feel her age and who was probably suffering from rheumatism in her legs. But Annie made no complaint.

As the sound of her footsteps faded along the landing, Matt and Jackie came in for their breakfasts. They had been out on the fells very early, rounding up some of the ewes for a routine health check.

'You know,' Matt was saying as they went to wash their hands, 'I think poor old Nell's coming to t'end of her days. She wasn't as sharp as she usually is, I've noticed she's been slowing down lately. Mebbe it's time we were thinking of a pup, summat that'll learn from Nell. I mean, she must be pretty ancient now. She's been on the go for years.'

'A bit like you, eh?' grinned Jackie. 'Not as young as you were or as young as you'd like to be!'

'We'll have less of that cheek!' and Matt playfully clipped Jackie over the ear, then added, 'What? No Grandad yet? He must have had a good night!'

'He was making merry when I saw him,' Jackie smiled. 'Having a right good celebration.'

'Ma's taken him a cup of tea,' Pat told them. 'Now, Jackie, does this arrival mean you want a second breakfast or just a cup of tea? I'm doing eggs and bacon for Grandad.'

'Working on those fells gives you an appetite, eh, Matt?' he chuckled. 'Wouldn't say no to some bacon and eggs, Mum.'

'You eat like a horse, Jackie. Matt, how about you?'

'I've had mine, but a mug o' tea and a slice of toast and marmalade wouldn't be amiss. It'll save bothering Dolly – she'll be seeing to young Sam now.'

'One full breakfast, one mug of tea, toast and marmalade coming up,' smiled Pat.

'Jack gone then, has he?' Matt settled at the table, as Pat poured his mug of tea and slipped a slice of brown bread into the toaster.

'He's gone to see some heifers at Hotten Mart,' she said. 'He's going up to Skipdale an' all, to collect some dry-cleaning for me. He's taken Sandie in, so he set off a bit earlier than he intended; it saved her bothering with the bus.'

'Ah, well, me and Jackie'll just have to manage without him,' and there was just a hint of reluctant acceptance in Matt's voice.

Jack had been away a lot in recent weeks; time and time again, he had found excuses for popping into Hotten, and on more than one occasion at the Mart Matt had seen him in very close conversation with the pretty Karen Moore. It had come to worry Matt, but at this stage he kept his suspicions to himself. After all, Karen was assistant auctioneer in the Hotten Mart office and so, if Jack was thinking of expanding his herd of Friesians, it was natural they'd talk and work together. But Matt felt this was more than a business liaison. Karen was a most attractive woman, and there was the time Jack had dressed up in his best suit to go to Hotten –

something he *never* did as a rule, even when seeing his bank manager.

Matt allowed his thoughts to fade as Pat busied herself with bacon and eggs for Grandad and Jackie. He collected the toast from the toaster and spread it with a generous layer of butter and marmalade.

As they concentrated on their meal, they could hear Ma's slow descent of the stairs, and then the door opened and she came into the kitchen. Her face showed clear signs of distress, but it was nothing to do with her rheumatism – she was still carrying Grandad's cup of tea.

'Ma?' Pat hurried to her, taking the cup, which was now rattling in its saucer. 'Ma, are you all right?'

Annie, close to tears, shook her head and supported herself with her hands against the table.

'It's Dad,' she said simply as she settled on a chair. For a long moment, no one said anything, because the unspoken message in her face was so awful to comprehend, but then Matt asked, 'Ma, you can't mean it . . .?'

'Aye, I can. I've seen it before, with my mother. Now it's Dad. In bed, during the night,' said Annie. 'No fuss, no pain. He's just passed away. He'll be at peace now, I know. But I can't really believe it's happened . . . it was so . . . well, unexpected, so sudden . . . There was no warning, nothing,' and then she began to weep.

For what seemed an eternity, no one said anything, each occupied with his or her own thoughts and concerns, none wanting to believe this terrible news.

'I'd best call t'doctor.' Matt took the initiative. 'I'll ring from home.'

He hurried round to his cottage, which was attached to the farmhouse. Annie could be wrong, it could be a coma or something similar, so a doctor's urgent presence was essential.

'Jackie, you find summat to do outside,' suggested Pat. 'I'll see to Ma.'

Jackie left in a daze; he had no idea what to do or what to say, and so he returned to the sheep and tried to interest himself in his work. But it was impossible to concentrate on the morning's tasks; he could not help thinking of Grandad last night, so happy and lively, so full of fun and pride. So instead of trying to work, Jackie went to the Skilbecks' cottage where he found Matt alone.

'Is there owt I can do?' he asked, his face a picture of sorrow.

'Aye, see if you can find Jack,' Matt told him. 'I've rung the surgery at Hotten, a doctor's coming straightaway. You use this phone – I'll get back to Ma and Pat. And somebody will have to tell Joe. That'd be best coming from Jack, eh? I'll find Dolly – she'll be out feeding up somewhere. Hen run I reckon, showing young Sam how she feeds hens and collects eggs.'

As Matt hurried off, Jackie picked up the telephone and rang Hotten Mart.

Hotten Mart was busy with the weekly intake of cattle as their owners inspected and prepared them for sale, while examining others with a view to potential purchase. The place was noisy, bustling

9

with farmers, vehicles and moving animals. Sandie Merrick, acting as a clerical assistant in the auctioneer's office, heard the ringing telephone and was tempted to ignore it. It was the third call this morning and Karen hadn't appeared yet; she was late again. Normally on a busy market day, she and Karen came in early to get a good start before the demands of the day began to materialise. So where was she today?

Cursing under her breath, Sandie picked up the receiver. 'Hotten Mart.'

'Sandie?' asked the anxious voice.

'Yes,' and she paused a moment, then asked, 'Jackie, is that you?'

'Aye, er, is Jack around?'

She hesitated before replying; the tone of Jackie's voice suggested that something was wrong, and at the same time she did not wish to fuel any speculation about her own suspicions of Jack. As she thought for those few seconds of what to say, she recalled the times Jack and Karen had had close conversations, cups of coffee together and hushed telephone discussions.

On more than one occasion, there had been calls for Karen at the office, calls that Sandie had answered before transferring them, and she'd been sure the voice had been Jack's . . . and today, Jack was in Hotten, ostensibly to visit the Mart, and Karen had not come in yet. Were they meeting somewhere?

'Sandie?' Jackie repeated. 'You there?'

'Sorry,' she apologised for her momentary lapse. 'Somebody came in.' She lied easily, uncertain of what to say next. 'What was it you wanted? Jack, you said?'

'Aye,' he sounded miserable. 'Can you find him?'

'Is it important?' she countered, wondering if all Jackie wanted was for Jack to get him a part for his motor cycle while in Hotten. 'I'm alone in the office and it's our busy time, Karen's not in and Mr Golding's down in the ring . . .'

'You'll have to find him, Sandie.' There was a clear note of despair in Jackie's voice now. 'You really will.'

'Jackie?' She now realised his call was serious. 'Jackie, what is it?'

'Grandad,' he said hoarsely. 'He's dead, Sandie. In bed. Annie found him . . . when she took his tea up . . . Matt's got the doctor in . . . you've got to find Jack, Sandie . . . tell him to get himself back home and never mind the cows.'

'Shall I come . . .?' she suggested.

'No, no need. Honest. It's best we keep away just now.'

'I'll see if I can find him,' she promised. 'How's Annie?'

'Upset, she found him. She's calm enough, but she's taken it badly, finding him like she did. I mean, he was in such a good mood last night . . . '

'Leave it to me, I'll see if I can find Jack,' and she replaced the telephone, hoping she had not sounded too curt. She loved old Sam Pearson as if he was her own grandfather, which, of course, he wasn't; he had been so wonderful as she was settling in at Emmerdale. He had known things were not easy for Sandie after her mother's divorce from Tom followed by her marriage to Jack. She'd been glad of his friendship and compassion. For a moment or two she sat with her own sad thoughts, and then a farmer came in.

'I've a couple of bullocks to be entered today,' he said.

'Just a moment, Mr Bradley.' She went across to the counter and opened the register. 'Now, what breed are they?'

For the next few minutes, Sandie was rushed off her feet with a surge of phone calls and visitors, and then, in a moment of peace, she rang Karen's home number. If Karen wasn't in the office, she must be at her flat; but if she was ill, why hadn't she rung in to say so? Sandie recalled Jack's parting words when he dropped her at the Mart this morning: 'Just going to park the Land Rover,' he'd said. 'Then I'll go and see what's on offer in the ring.' And from that time, she'd not seen him – or Karen. She hung on to the end of the line as the telephone rang in Karen's flat. But there was no reply.

Sandie replaced the receiver, wondering if she dare leave her own office for five or ten minutes to seek Jack. She peered out of the window and saw that no one appeared to be heading her way, and so she rushed out, locking the door behind her. She made for the ring, passing the car park on the way, but saw no sign of the Emmerdale Land Rover. In the ring, she stood at the back of the circle of buyers and sellers, peering at the sea of faces. Mr Golding was busy auctioning a fine black Aberdeen Angus bull, but there was no sign of Jack.

She knew that when he came to the Mart he

usually stood near the green pillar, just to the left of the auctioneer's dais, but he wasn't there today. She left the ring and decided to check the little café used by the market visitors for coffee and snacks. Jack was not there either and now she had to return to her office.

A little queue had formed outside and one of the farmers grumbled, 'Now then, lass, been out for coffee, have we? Some of us are here on business, working tha knaws . . .'

'So am I, Mr Milburn,' she snapped as she unlocked the door to let them in. 'You haven't seen Jack Sugden have you? I want to find him urgently. I've looked everywhere.'

'Never clapped eyes on him today, lass,' he said. 'Now, I've some Red Polls to fit in today if we can. Six good milkers . . .'

Sandie began to wish that today could have been cancelled.

Somehow, she muddled through the morning, coping with callers at the office and dozens of telephone calls. She repeatedly dialled Karen's number without success. Jackie rang back twice, his calls echoing the distress at Emmerdale Farm; each time he asked if she'd located Jack and each time she had to say, 'No, not yet.' Fortunately, Mr Golding was fully occupied in the sales ring and he had not yet missed Karen; normally, if one of the girls was absent for any doubtful reason, the other would cheerfully cover up for her but Sandie was now pondering about the ethics of covering for a woman who seemed to be having an affair with her stepfather. Sandie's reactions required careful thought. But was Karen really involved with Jack? Even Sandie, close as she was to both Karen and Jack, did not know the true answer.

The rest of the morning vanished in a haze of hectic work and she found herself with little time to dwell upon sad thoughts of Sam Pearson or to make further efforts to find Jack.

Lunchtime offered blessed relief from the pressures of the office and she decided to go into the town for a break instead of buying a sandwich to eat at her desk. Mr Golding had already broken for his lunch and was at the Black Bull with a couple of his regular clients, and so Sandie decided it was time to lock the office door. First, she would ring Emmerdale to see if Jack had returned, but even as she picked up the telephone, she noticed the Emmerdale Land Rover in the square.

It eased to a halt at the far side of the market, close to a group of cattle trucks near the vets' surgery, and from the security of her office she saw that Jack was at the wheel with Karen at his side. They were talking earnestly, then Karen stepped out and disappeared behind the line of cattle trucks. She dashed out, waving her arms to attract Jack's attention before he could drive off again. Sandie knew Karen was deliberately taking a round-about route back to the office in the hope of avoiding any observant eyes.

'Jack!' Sandie called as she ran. 'Jack, don't go.'

He noticed her and waved in response, then drew down the window. 'Hi, Sandie.' His voice tried to sound cheerful. 'I was just coming to find you, to see if you'd let me buy you lunch.'

She ignored his offer. 'Jack, where the hell have you been? We've been looking all over the place for you, the market, the town, Jackie's been ringing . . .'

'Summat wrong, is there?' He flushed as he realised the folly of his actions that morning, and tried to make light of it by saying, 'Jackie having trouble with that tractor, is he? Won't it start? It's time we had a new 'un.'

As Sandie stood at the side of the vehicle, her face a mask of anger and sorrow, Jack realised something was seriously wrong.

'Sorry,' he continued. 'I'm sorry, Sandie. What's up? It *is* summat serious, isn't it?'

'It's Grandad.' Her voice had a chill to it, an echo of her own feelings about his suspected behaviour. 'Jackie's been ringing . . . Ma found him this morning. Just after we left home, Jack. In bed. Jack, your grandad has died.'

'Grandad?' He climbed out of the vehicle and stood at her side, his face showing the guilt and embarrassment he felt at the awful situation in which he now found himself. He could read Sandie's face – she knew he'd spent the entire morning with Karen; though she could not know that they had been in Karen's flat, ignoring the phone. Karen had hoped that Mr Golding would be fully occupied and that, if necessary, Sandie would cover for her.

'He passed away in his sleep, Jack. Very peacefully during the night. Ma found him when she took his cup of tea up. They want you back at the farm.'

'Oh my God . . .'

He clambered back into his Land Rover and drove

15

away, with Sandie watching to see if he would find Karen before returning home; he didn't. Instead, he took the road to Beckindale.

Sandie continued into Hotten town centre; she needed the break, and this afternoon she would inform Karen of the news. She wondered what reaction it would have on the woman she had once regarded as a friend.

The sudden death of Sam Pearson stunned the residents of Beckindale and the surrounding district. Friends and former colleagues rang to express their sorrow. Within hours of the news breaking, callers brought cards and flowers in an attempt to comfort Annie and offer condolences to the family. At this stage, Annie seemed bravely in control; it had not yet sunk in that she would never again see her father in his favourite fireside chair, or working in his shed, or pottering among his vegetables and flowers.

Dr Potter from the Hotten practice had come swiftly to the bedside, and said Sam had been dead for some hours. Death was from natural causes, he had explained to the family, and Sam had never been in any pain or distress. It had been a perfect way to close a happy, contented life and this did give some reassurance to Annie. The last thing she had wanted was for her father to suffer in those final moments.

When Jack returned, shortly before two o'clock, Pat met him outside the door and hissed, 'And where the hell have you been? We've been looking everywhere. Jackie, Matt, me, Sandie . . .'

'Hotten,' he said. 'The Mart. Looking at heifers.'

'Sandie's searched high and low, Jack, and you weren't there.'

'I went to the bank, luv, but I hadn't an appointment. I had to queue, I had to go back several times from the Mart because MacCauley was busy; managers are allus busy on mart day. That'd be when Sandie was looking for me. Anyroad, how's Ma?'

'You'd best go in and find out,' Pat said frostily. She followed him inside where his mother was sitting in the parlour, pale but composed.

'Ma,' was all he said.

'Jack, it's all over. Poor Dad . . . he never knew a thing.'

'You found him?'

'Aye, Jack, I did.'

She told him her story as he sat at her side clutching her hand and he apologised for not being there in a time of such need. He excused himself by blaming his trips to the bank, and in these circumstances, no one quizzed him too closely. Yet even in the midst of family gloom and despair he could not stop his mind wandering back to his time with Karen this morning, in her flat and in her bed . . . He started guiltily.

'I'll set about the funeral arrangements,' he said, knowing that as the eldest male relative this was his duty.

'Ring Joe first, make sure he can come,' his mother asked, and then she stressed, 'I do want Joe to come to the funeral, Jack.'

'Aye, and he'll want to come,' he replied.

* * *

The funeral of Sam Pearson was arranged for 3pm the following Saturday at St Mary's Parish Church, Beckindale, and Jack made sure that notices appeared in the *Yorkshire Post* and *Hotten Courier*. The service was arranged late in the day to allow Joe to fly in from France in the morning, and to permit the essential farmwork, such as first milking, to be completed. These arrangements were ideal because Joe could not get away any earlier due to important commitments at the NY Estate Office near Tours. His flight was due to arrive at the Leeds-Bradford Airport at 10.30am. If the plane was on time, he would be at Emmerdale for lunch, a feat of travel that would have astounded his grandfather. Sam Pearson could never have understood that someone could be in Paris one morning and at his funeral in Yorkshire the same day.

Annie kept busy with her arrangements, especially those for the funeral tea which would follow the church service. In the tradition of the Yorkshire Dales it would be a ham tea, and with the anticipation of a large congregation, she knew she could expect a full house as the dalesfolk gathered afterwards at the farm. Old Sam Pearson had had many friends.

With Dolly, Pat and Sandie helping, Annie was fully occupied while Jack planned matters affecting the funeral service and the interment. He organised the bearers, transport for some of the more elderly mourners, the seating arrangements at church and later at the farm, and a range of ancilliary matters like where to put the mass of floral tributes, and what drinks should accompany the funeral tea.

During the preparatory work, Sandie proved an immense help, particularly in the support she gave to Annie, but Jackie had no idea what was expected of him. In the days preceding the funeral, he kept out of the house as much as possible, finding lots of work on the farm to occupy him through the long hours as the others went about the business of coping with a death in the family.

Pat, though with one eye constantly on Jack during these dark moments, found herself working hard, and for a while she forgot her worries about his secretive activities and unexplained absences from the farm.

Meanwhile, Matt and Dolly had the difficult task of explaining to young Sam about Grandad's death. Matt believed they should not try to conceal the truth in any way – he felt they should explain that old people do die and that Grandad had gone to heaven. In a mind as young as Sam's this would not mean a lot, but Dolly's main concern was that her son should not grow up remembering nothing of dear old Sam Pearson. Matt felt that this would be solved in some way because the family would continue to talk about the dead man in a loving way; young Sam would always be surrounded by memories of the man he knew as Grandad.

And so the day of the funeral dawned. It was a chilly morning in early November. At his mother's instigation, Jack rang the Leeds-Bradford Airport to see if Joe's flight was likely to be delayed, and everyone was relieved to learn that it would be on time. Pleased to be away from the house for a while, Pat drove to meet him.

In spite of the pressures upon her in the precious hours before the funeral, Annie made sure she met Joe the moment he stepped from the car in the yard outside the kitchen. Tears of sorrow turned into tears of joy as she hugged her youngest son, holding him in a tight embrace as the others took Joe's luggage indoors.

'Hey, Ma!' Joe gasped. 'Put me down!'

'Oh, Joe.' She brushed a tear from her eye after kissing him warmly. 'It's so good to see you, so good . . .'

'I'm sorry it's taken Grandad . . . well . . . a funeral, to get me here.'

'Shush!' She released him from her powerful embrace and linked her arm through his as she walked him to the house. 'I'm just glad you came. The others are waiting inside. We can talk later.'

'Are you coping?' Joe asked, with concern in his voice, as he reached the kitchen door. He stood back to allow his mother to enter.

'Aye,' she said. 'I am. I miss him, we all do, but knowing you were coming has helped me. How's things in France?'

'Later, Ma.' He followed her into the kitchen. 'There's time for a long chat when all this is over. So come on, let's get moving, I'm sure there's a lot to do.'

After a brief but warm welcome from everyone, Joe showered and changed into a dark suit, and joined his family in their sad preparations.

Jackie had bought a new suit too, a dark grey one which made him look older and smarter that he usually did, and he was accompanied by his newest girlfriend, the quiet but charming Alison Caswell whose family farmed higher in the dale. She had helped him to get ready, giving him the valuable reassurance that he needed. With the funeral service about to commence, she was at his side in the church as preparations were made to carry the coffin forward to the altar. Jack, Joe and Matt were bearers, along with three cousins on Sam's side of the family, and the packed church, with its masses of floral tributes, echoed to the sound of the tolling bell. Throughout the village, curtains along the route of the funeral procession had been closed and all the business premises in Beckindale had shut up for the afternoon as a mark of respect for Sam.

'I've never been to a funeral before,' Jackie whispered to Alison, the concern showing in his eyes.

'I have,' Alison told him quietly. 'My own grandad and grandma's. They're not easy, you'll be more upset than you realise, Jackie, but don't be ashamed of it.'

'I'll be all right.' He tried to show some youthful bravado, but inwardly, he had no idea what to expect.

Then the bells stopped.

Everyone rose to their feet and Jackie was tempted to turn his head to see what was happening at the back of the church, for he could hear the sound of shuffling footsteps. He realised that the vicar, the Reverend Donald Hinton, was now standing before the altar. Jackie suddenly saw that everyone else, including Alison, was bowing their heads and so he did likewise. Then the organist struck a chord and the choir and congregation began to sing:

21

Now the labourer's task is o'er;
Now the battle day is past;
Now upon the farther shore
Lands the voyager at last.
Father, in thy gracious keeping
Leave we now thy servant sleeping.

Quite suddenly, a lump came to Jackie's throat and he found himself sorely missing dear old Sam. He bit his lips as the continuing words of the hymn registered in his mind and Sam's coffin came to rest before the altar.

As the vicar began the sombre prayers, Jackie found himself unable to watch the proceedings. He knelt with his head bowed as the impressive words of the burial service filled the quiet church.

Many of the mourners came back to Emmerdale Farm afterwards. Jack, Joe and Jackie were responsible for filling glasses, while Pat, Dolly and Sandie ensured that everyone had sufficient to eat. Annie supervised the entire operation. People stood in small groups, talking about how fond they'd been of Sam, relating delightful tales about their memories of him – the vicar had stories of Sam and his flute-playing at the Christmas pantomimes, Amos and Seth remembered battles with carrots and cabbages at the produce shows, and one old friend recalled throwing Sam into the village pond during a tussle over the love of a woman – Annie's mother. Sam had lost that particular battle – but he did eventually win the hand of the woman he loved.

Reminiscences of this kind soon had the gathering

laughing and joking, and the constant flow of alcohol served only to intensify the jollifications. Annie moved from room to room, renewing acquaintance with people she had not seen for years, remembering past friendships and other family gatherings. Jack also circulated, making introductions where necessary, checking that no one was left alone and generally ensuring that the funeral tea was a success.

Then, quite unexpectedly, he found Jackie standing all alone in a corner of the passage – Alison was helping Sandie with more plates of sandwiches and cakes. Jack approached him with a jug of beer and offered to fill his empty glass. But Jackie put his hand over it to indicate he did not want any more and Jack noticed the sadness in the lad's face.

'You all right?' Jack asked.

Jackie was almost in tears. 'I never thought it would be like this,' he said. 'All this laughing and joking, folks telling tales about Grandad and that. It's more like a party.'

'Funerals are never easy,' Jack said. 'Relations and folks claiming friendship turn up after years without coming near the spot and expect us to feed 'em and entertain 'em. I suppose it does summat for family bonding, but I'm not sure what. Come tomorrow, they'll have forgotten all about this funeral, what it's supposed to mean and so on, and they'll find another to attend. Grandad'll be nowt but a memory, Jackie. But don't get upset – that never helps.'

Jackie shrugged. 'I think I'll go outside for a bit.'

'Farewells are rotten, eh?' Jack said. 'Especially when they're so permanent.'

'I loved him, Jack, I really did,' and Jackie went out of the back door, sniffing back his tears.

Jack returned to his duties and as he surveyed the packed rooms of Emmerdale Farm, it crossed his mind that it would be far nicer to be walking the banks of the River Aire with Karen. He shrugged the thought away, his mind returning to Jackie. 'We all miss you, Grandad,' he whispered to himself as he pushed through the packed room towards his mother and Joe.

Chapter Two

When Joe came to the farm the next morning, having slept at Demdyke Cottage, there was no sign of his mother. Sandie was having a lie-in, Jack was in the mistle and Pat was at the sink, washing the breakfast pots and listening to the morning service on the radio. The house still bore signs of the funeral tea – some forgotten glasses on the mantelshelf, a pile of clean plates waiting to be stored somewhere, the cards of condolence on the windowledge and various plates of uneaten salad and sandwiches.

'Morning, Pat. Where's Ma?'

'Hi, Joe. She went out for a walk,' smiled Pat. 'I said I'd clean up in here, she's going to church at eleven, she said. Was it something special? I'll see if I can find her.'

'Just thought I'd pop in to see if she's all right,' he grinned.

'Yes, she's fine; she snapped Dolly's head off this morning for asking that! She says everybody's asking how she is and she's OK, she's coping very well and seems quite content to be with her own thoughts and memories just now.'

'I'm off to Home Farm for a chat with Alan Turner over coffee this morning,' he said. 'May as well do a bit of business while I'm here. I'll see if I can find Ma – and I won't ask how she is!'

Joe located his mother in Grandad's shed at the

top of the steps at the end of the house. She was lingering among the bits and pieces that Sam had accumulated – lengths of used timber, tins of paint, packets of nails and screws, brushes, tools of every kind, balls of string, old newspapers and a whole host of other ancient and rather useless things.

'Hi, Ma.' He sounded his usual cheery self. 'Going to tidy this spot up, are you?'

'It needs it!' she laughed. 'Dad hoarded all sorts, didn't he? He never threw anything away in case it came in useful later – I once heard him say that everything comes in useful once every seven years!'

'What's this, then?' Joe picked up a partially completed toy.

'A truck for young Sam. He said he'd make it for Sam's birthday, but never got it finished. It was going to be a four-wheel truck with a tipper on the back, for little Sam to push around with loads in. It'll never get finished now.'

'Jack might have a go!' said Joe, not really meaning it.

'Young Jackie more like. Dad was often showing him how to make things. Jack seems busy with his own thoughts these days, he's hardly ever here now.'

'I thought he seemed a bit preoccupied at the funeral,' observed Joe.

'Aye, he seems to be living in summat of a dream world, Joe. I don't know what's got into him lately.'

'He coped well with the funeral,' Joe said. 'Got things organised very efficiently and looked after everybody.'

'Yes, I needed him then, Joe. He can be very kind.'

'Things going well with the farm, are they?' Joe asked his mother. 'Jackie settling in and working well? He was fast asleep when I left Demdyke.'

'Things are up and down, Joe. We had a good harvest and Jack's got some fine cows now; he wants more, mind. He's never satisfied; he intends having the best herd of Friesians hereabouts. He says that'll be his legacy for the family – he means Jackie by that, I reckon. Anyway, you'll be off back to France soon, eh?'

'Tomorrow. I've got to see Alan Turner this morning on a bit of business. I'll be back for Christmas, though. I've promised myself a few weeks here over Christmas and New Year.'

'You'll be here for dinner today, won't you?'

'You bet I will! Didn't you know I decided to stay here over the weekend just to sample Emmerdale roast beef and Yorkshire pudding? They don't have Sunday dinners like that in France, you know – over there, it's all frogs' legs and garlic!'

Annie laughed. 'Get away with you! Anyway, here's one job I've got lined up to do. Clean out this shed, and then have a go at Dad's bedroom – that's full of papers and rubbish an' all! It'll need a right sorting out!'

'Must be off,' smiled Joe, kissing her suddenly. 'See you at dinner time.'

He trotted down the stone steps and hurried away towards Home Farm. Annie watched him leave and knew that his cheerful presence was helping her cope with the loss of her father. When she returned to the kitchen, Dolly had come in with young Sam and was chatting to Pat.

'Hi, Ma,' This time, Dolly refrained from asking how she was. Annie acknowledged her and smiled at the youngster.

'Have you explained to him – about Dad?' she asked Dolly as she settled in her chair.

'Matt tried to tell him but I don't think he understands,' Dolly admitted. 'Matt said Grandad had gone to see Jesus and that he would never return, and one day we would all join him.'

Annie smiled again at this thought. 'Aye,' she agreed. 'That's true enough. We'll still be one big happy family, but in another world.'

And as they talked, young Sam toddled across the kitchen and climbed into Grandpa's fireside chair. Annie was amused at the sight of the little lad settling down in Sam's favourite seat.

'You know,' she said, 'nobody sat in that chair yesterday – nobody's used it since Dad's death, in fact. And now young Sam's making his claim to it. I reckon Dad would have liked that.'

Dolly regarded her son with fondness. 'Aye, they got on well, didn't they? The two Sams.' Then after a pause, she said, 'Come on, young Sam, Daddy'll be in for his coffee soon.'

He climbed down from the chair and followed his mum out of the kitchen. Annie felt comforted by the fact that life at Emmerdale was continuing. As Pat busied herself with the Sunday dinner, Annie went to find her hat and best coat for church, but met Sandie on the stairs.

'I thought I'd come to church with you?' Sandie made the statement sound like a question.

'That's nice,' and Annie was pleased at this suggestion.

Pat, left alone with her thoughts in the farm kitchen, realised that the time between Grandad's death and the funeral had been one of peace for her. During those few days, Jack had been at home with her and the family instead of disappearing without reason into Hotten, or wherever he had been going in recent weeks. Although he had been very quiet with her, there had been none of those furtive telephone calls, no late nights and no excuses for being away during the day.

Over and over again, Pat had tried to tell herself that there could not be another woman in Jack's life; she had made herself believe that his black moods and unhappy behaviour were due to some private difficult time he was going through. Perhaps it was a financial problem that he would not discuss with anyone, or maybe it was something connected with the expansion schemes he so dearly wished for Emmerdale. His depression might be the result of his natural restlessness, his desire to find some other absorbing way of life of the kind he had sampled in Rome. But Jack was always so reticent about his inner thoughts and wishes; he seldom spoke to her or to anyone else about his problems and desires. But, by reflecting upon all aspects of his recent behaviour, she had to accept that there were huge gaps and many inconsistencies in his stories, certainly enough to give her rise for concern.

She could not help thinking of the time he'd spent two nights away from home. He'd gone to the Royal

Show at Stoneleigh, and had stayed at an hotel in Kenilworth when normally he'd have driven there and back in one day. In other circumstances, that would not have raised any worry in her mind, but when reflecting upon the entirety of his odd behaviour, it could be part of a larger jigsaw, an indication of a liaison with someone else. She shuddered at the thought and felt awful for even thinking such a thing of her husband. But there were other factors, things she could not ignore.

There were times his clothes had smelled of curry or cigarette smoke and she was sure that sometimes his jacket and shirts had borne traces of make-up which wasn't hers. And there was a new shirt which had mysteriously appeared in the laundry basket; when she had spoken to him about it, he said he'd bought it in Hotten on impulse because it had taken his fancy. That was something Jack had never done – he'd never bought himself a shirt, a tie or even socks. He'd always relied on people to buy those things for him, at Christmas or for birthdays.

But in spite of all these warning signs, and in spite of Jack's recent reluctance to make love to her, she continued in her hope that he was not being unfaithful; she wanted to believe he had problems of another kind, problems they'd one day discuss as man and wife. Pat tried to make herself believe this.

On the Monday morning after the funeral, she climbed early from her bed and made a cup of tea for Jack. It was not his morning for milking, which meant he could have a short lie-in, and as she carried in the cup, she smiled down at him. He lay in the depths of their bed, the blankets up to his shoulders, and at the sound of her at his side, he opened his eyes and stifled a yawn. 'Hello, what's this?'

'Tea in bed.' She tried to appear bright and breezy and hoped her behaviour did not indicate anything of her mental turmoil. 'I thought you deserved a bit of mollycoddling after all the work you did for the funeral.'

'Oh, ta,' and she placed it beside him on the bedside cabinet. But he did not drink it; instead, he pretended to be more tired than he really was and curled up again beneath the clothes. Disappointed, she turned away from him.

'It's gone eight,' she added coldly as she went across to the dressing table and settled before the mirror. Hurt by his apparent rejection of her warmth, she began to brush her auburn hair with long, slow strokes, frustrated and hurt by his lack of interest in her. She brushed for a long time, eventually seeing Jack rise from the blankets, sit up and lean back on the headboard to pick up his cup of tea. He drank it slowly, all the time watching her; she could see him in the mirror and wondered what his thoughts were. Did he still find her attractive in spite of ageing . . . in spite of having two grown-up children . . . in spite of her being grandmother to Sandie's illegitimate baby girl . . .?

After a few moments of this, she rose from the dressing table and made for the door. 'I won't ask what you are thinking,' she said. 'You'll only say "nothing"!'

He did say nothing, nothing at all, and she left the room upset by his dismissive action. Downstairs, she

tried to appear cheerful as she prepared his breakfast, and as Jack arrived at the table, Jackie came in
from milking. He washed his hands as Annie mashed
the tea. Sandie had gone to work and Pat and Annie
were thinking already of Christmas.

'We'll have to be sorting out our Christmas card
list,' Annie was saying to Pat. 'It always gets left till
it becomes a rush and by then we've dozens of cards
in and none sent out.'

'We'll do it one evening,' said Jack, as if the
remark had been addressed to him.

Pat responded, 'You always say that, Jack, and it
always gets missed, year after year. When you say
an evening, do you mean *this* evening?'

'Er, no,' he said. 'Not tonight, tomorrow mebbe.'

'Why not tonight?' demanded Pat, the suspicions
arising in her.

'I've got to go to Hotten,' he said and she noticed
that he did not look directly at her. 'I said I'd chat
to Eric Hall about a replacement tractor; that 'un of
ours is on its last legs, it's almost an antique.'

'You can say that again!' chipped in Jackie. 'I
reckon it's only the muck that's holding it together!'

'Yeh, well, Eric reckons he knows where I can get
a good second-hand one and asked me to discuss it
over a pint.'

'Does it have to be tonight?' Pat demanded.
'You're out most nights now, and it's always without
me . . . We never go anywhere together, Jack, not
now.'

'Pat!' he snapped and then stopped short of
making any further comment when he realised
Annie was watching him with more than her usual

32

interest. 'Look, it's the only time Eric can see me. We're meeting at the Black Bull.'

'Then I can come,' she said.

'If you want,' he tried to sound reasonable. 'But it'll bore you silly; besides, I thought you were going to get started on the Christmas card list.'

In the moment of strained silence that followed, Annie said, 'Let men do men's work, Pat,' and for a moment, Pat wondered if she was being over-sensitive about Jack's outings.

'I'll do the card list,' she capitulated. 'And then there's our own present list to make out,' she added for good measure.

'Tomorrow night, like I said,' and he took the plate of eggs and bacon she had prepared. It had been kept warm on the Aga and smelt delicious. 'That's a promise.'

Following this exchange, there was a long silence in the kitchen. Annie was clearly aware of the increasing tension between Jack and Pat, but young Jackie seemed oblivious to the undercurrents. He was tucking into a massive breakfast, his second that morning, and was reading *Motor Cycle News*. His greatest desire was to own a brand new high-powered Japanese bike. He gulped down his meal and hurried out. When Jack finished his meal, he left the table without a word, and without kissing Pat or thanking her. She knew he had gone to the mistle, for it would have to be swilled out now that milking was over.

Annie watched her.

'You'll be helping him swill out?' She put the question as if it were a piece of motherly advice.

33

'I suppose so.' But Pat's tone of voice lacked any hint of enthusiasm.

'Pat,' said Annie. 'If Jack's having a tough time, he'll need you around him, luv. You can't shut him out of your life even if he's shut you out of his.'

'Oh, Ma, he won't talk. You know him, how deep he is. There is summat, and I don't know what it is or what to do about it. He . . . well . . . he just seems as if he doesn't need me any more.'

'Course he needs you, Pat. You mustn't go about thinking otherwise. Mebbe he's not showing it very well just now, but if a man's having worries, he does need his wife. You can be sure of that.'

'I wish I was so sure, Ma,' and Pat collected her overall and went out. In the yard, she halted for a moment, drew in a deep breath and went across to the mistle. Jack was already at work and she could hear the hissing of the hosepipe as he washed the floor with floods of ice-cold water. Without a word, she picked up the yard brush with its head of thick bristles and began to brush away the mess. Matt came in to help too, having enjoyed his coffee break, and for the next quarter of an hour they worked in silence, with Matt fully aware of the growing rift between Jack and Pat. But Matt being Matt, he made no comment about it.

That Monday morning, Joe popped in to Emmerdale Farm to say goodbye to everyone before returning to France. Annie had steeled herself for Joe's departure, but she lost the battle to hide her misery at losing him yet again and dissolved in tears. The others allowed her a few moments alone with Joe in the parlour, and then said their farewells. They watched his taxi turn from the lane into the main road, but Annie could not bear this; she went inside to be alone with her thoughts.

She purged her sorrow by spending the following days in a whirl of bustling activity. She began to clear out Grandad's room, disposing of his clothes and many other possessions while retaining items like family photographs, some of his personal treasures and souvenirs. There was a war medal, a collection of £.s.d. coins and some old books and diaries, including a handwritten gardening diary that Sam had maintained for years. It was then that she recalled his notebook of country lore – some years ago, he'd started to compile a notebook of country weather-sayings, planting times, saints' days and so forth. Where had that got to? She hoped it had not been destroyed. No, there it was, at the bottom of the wardrobe.

In addition to this activity, there were all the Christmas preparations. There was the cake and the pudding to make, the shopping to do in Harrogate or York, the preparations for the family Christmas dinner and, on top of all this, there was the seasonal work on the farm, a major part of which was the plucking of the Emmerdale Christmas geese to sell in Hotten Mart.

For Annie Sugden, the coming weeks were to be very busy indeed and the planning helped her over-come the lingering sense of loss she was experiencing over Grandad's death and Joe's departure. She hoped Joe would come home for Christmas as promised; she'd had so little time to talk with him, to find out more about his life in France and whether he was really happy there. His time at Emmerdale, brought about through sadness and loss, now seemed so ephemeral and distant. But she could not dwell on Joe for long, for there were more serious matters to concern her.

There was Jack and Pat's marriage for a start.

It was increasingly clear to Annie that things were not right, and that Jack's treatment of Pat was bordering on disdain and even neglect.

She smiled when she thought of young Jackie, though. His romance with Alison Caswell was strengthening and met with the approval of both families. Alison was a country girl through and through, the daughter of a successful local farmer, and a girl with no pretensions or wild dreams beyond her capabilities. Practical and full of commonsense, everyone knew she would be a most suitable wife for Jackie. There was the question of whether he would bring her to Emmerdale for Christmas dinner, or whether he would be invited to join the Caswells at their home. Jackie seemed to think he would have to go there, which would mean a depletion of the family at Annie's table, although he did suggest bringing Alison to Emmerdale on Boxing Day.

Pat was pleased her son might visit the Caswells, for it would reinforce the links between Jackie and Alison. She was relieved, however, that she would have Sandie at home. Sandie did not, at this stage, have a serious boyfriend.

At the back of her mind Pat wondered how and where Jack would spend his Christmas. In his present mood, it seemed that her Christmas would be very miserable and she was not looking forward to the conflicts it could bring. She shed many secret tears in the weeks preceding the day but was determined not to let her worries spoil the celebrations.

She made a vow to do her best to be cheerful and to sort out Jack's problems before they became too much of a burden – for him, as well as for everyone else. Furthermore, she knew she must be very supportive towards Annie, for this would the first Christmas without Grandad. However, Pat began to dread the holiday.

With the first snow of the winter high on the fells, the atmosphere of Christmas intensified; the frost in the dale covered the ponds and waterways with a thin layer of ice and coated the bare hedgerows and trees with beautiful strands of glistening white tinsel. In Beckindale, the villagers were preparing for the holiday; the local inn, the Woolpack, with its resident licensee and proprietor, Mr Amos Brearly, and his partner, Mr Henry Wilks, were looking forward to a busy and hospitable time, while the Vicar of Beckindale, the Reverend Donald Hinton, was in the throes of producing the annual pantomime. This year, it was to be a variation on *The Pirates of Penzance*, with Alan Turner, the bumptious manager of NY Estates, and Amos Brearly both wanting to play the Major General and Beckindale's residents taking the other parts.

It was with the pantomime in mind that the Reverend Hinton called upon Matt and Dolly Skilbeck as they were having their morning coffee. Both Dolly and Matt had discussed this probability, with

37

Matt saying he would be happy to help with the scenery and backstage work.

'I need four daughters for the Major General,' said Hinton over his mug of coffee. 'And, well, Dolly, it struck me that you would be very suitable as one of them, Ruth I felt.'

'It's all the singing.' She was far from confident about this proposal. 'I'd be very nervous.'

'Nonsense, I know you'd be just right. But look, I don't expect you to give me an answer straight away. Think about it. Now, I've a cassette with a recording of *Pirates* on it – Alan Turner has borrowed it for the time being, to study the Major General's role, and when he's finished, I'll bring it for you to listen to. And Matt, what about you?'

Matt chuckled. 'Nay, Vicar, you know my singing voice would spoil everybody's enjoyment. But I'll be happy to work behind the scenes as usual. Stagehand or summat. Painting scenery, bits of joinery, that sort of thing. You can count on me for that.'

'Good, well, we do need those skills, Matt. Now I must get round to see Jack and Pat. I have a part in mind for Jack, you know . . .'

'He's up the fields, Vicar, doing some walling,' Matt explained.

'Not to worry, I want a word with Pat and Annie anyway,' and he rose to leave the Skilbecks.

Matt escorted him to the door and said, 'They tell me you've persuaded young Jackie to join in, an' all?'

'Dolly and Sandie have assured me they'll get him down to the village hall for auditions,' he laughed as he departed. When he'd gone, Dolly gathered up

38

the mugs to wash them as Matt prepared to return to work, donning his heavy, warm clothes before heading up to the fell to inspect his wintering ewes.

'He won't have much luck with Jack, will he?' Dolly said.

'I wouldn't have thought so,' Matt responded.

'I mean,' Dolly was thoughtful, 'he's not got much time for the farm or his family these days, let alone things that are happening in the village.'

'It's nowt to do with us, luv,' said Matt quietly.

'Well, I think it is. It's upsetting Pat because she's not sure what's going on, although I reckon she has a good idea, and now Ma's beginning to realise there's summat not right. I've seen the way she's been looking at him recently. I mean, Matt, he could spoil their Christmas and ours, and it might be worse than that – you know as well as I do that he's seeing Karen Moore.'

'Who told you that?' Matt expressed some surprise at Dolly's revelation.

'Things get around, Matt, you can't keep things like that quiet for long round here. You knew, didn't you? I know you've been bothered about Jack.'

'Aye, well, you're right, Dolly. I've seen him at Hotten Mart with her, talking deep, if you know what I mean. When me and him's been there selling sheep or looking at cows, he's allus made a beeline for Karen, made excuses to be with her.'

'And Sandie's seen 'em as well,' Dolly added. 'She's sick about it all, Matt – after all, Karen is a workmate and her best friend, and it's her mother that Karen's deceiving . . . it's a rotten thing for

39

Sandie. You can see how it's affecting her – the poor lass doesn't know what to do.'

'What *can* she do?' Matt shrugged his shoulders. 'It might blow over, it's mebbe just an infatuation.'

'Shouldn't you have words with Jack?' Dolly suggested. 'He mebbe needs to talk to a friend.'

'It's not our concern, luv, much as I can see the harm he's doing and likely to do. You know what Jack's like, he never talks about his deep feelings, never lets others know what's going through his mind. But if he does want to talk, then I'll listen. But I'm not going to interfere.'

'You reckon it's best if we just leave it, then? To sort itself out?'

'Aye, I do. We might only make things worse if we stick our noses in.'

'But what about Pat?' Dolly asked. 'She's the one who's really going to get hurt; shouldn't somebody tell her or at least warn her what's happening under her nose?'

'Happen she just might know,' said Matt. 'Pat's not stupid and you can bet she has some idea what's going on – and she'll do her best to nip it in the bud.'

'So you think I shouldn't mention it to Pat?'

'Not unless she says summat first. If she wants to talk it over with somebody, she'll say so and I reckon you, or mebbe Sandie, will be the first she'll come to. She might not tell Ma, Jack being her son,' Matt advised. 'Well, I'd best be getting up to the fells. It could be blowing up for more snow up yonder by the look of that sky. I might fetch 'em down to the lower slopes for tonight. Tell you what, luv, when I

40

get back, I'll be ready for a slap-up hot dinner and summat very warm to drink!'

'It'll be ready,' promised Dolly, kissing him. And as Matt left for the cold work among his flock on the high fells, Dolly also considered how Jack's blossoming affair would affect Christmas at Emmerdale Farm.

Jack was also wondering how his deepening relationship with Karen would affect all of them. It was clear in his mind that Pat realised he was seeing another woman, even if she did not know who it was. He found himself hating himself for everything he did to Pat, every hurt that he inflicted upon her, and yet he found himself unable to break off his romance.

He needed Karen, he loved her too, he realised; it was more than just the sexual side of their relationship, although he did accept that that was both important and enjoyable. He felt an affinity with Karen; she was interested in him for his own sake, interested in his work and his life. He could talk to her, he could ramble on about trivialities, about his conservation ideals as well as the issues surrounding his work at Emmerdale. And she would listen to him. He reflected upon their moments in bed on Wednesday afternoons, which was Karen's half-day off, and realised that she really did love him too. He could not see how he could ever give up Karen.

'I'm going into Hotten,' he said to Pat one afternoon about a week before Christmas.

'What for?' she asked, the suspicion showing immediately in her voice. 'Meeting somebody?'

'No, just doing a bit of shopping,' he said. 'I always go into Hotten before Christmas to buy presents. You've never grumbled about it before. There's nothing wrong in that, is there?'

'You might have offered to take me,' she countered. 'I could have done with a shopping session in Hotten.'

'You'd spoil my surprise then,' he laughed uneasily. 'I'll go with you on Saturday, eh?'

Pat said nothing, but turned away and walked over to the sheep pens. Moments later, Jack left in the Land Rover.

In Hotten he met Karen. She had arranged to take half a day's holiday which was due to her for conducting a sale on a recent Saturday afternoon, and they met at her flat. She welcomed him in her negligée and, within moments, they were in her bedroom, hugging each other in the warmth of her bed.

'You got away all right?' she asked.

'I said I had some shopping to do,' he told her. 'And it's true. I want to buy you something special, something for Christmas, something that you really want.'

She kissed him as he caressed her, his warm hands giving joy to her as they relaxed together.

'I just want you,' she said. 'Nothing else.'

He kissed her. 'A nice piece of jewellery mebbe? Earrings? Something you'd not buy for yourself.'

'No, Jack. I can't buy you anything, can I? I can't give you a present that you'll have to explain to everyone, so you mustn't give me one.'

'You've given me yourself,' he said. 'No man

42

could ask for more than that. But I might think of summat!'

She snuggled in his arms and they lay together for a long, long time, two warm loving bodies wanting nothing more than one another.

'Jack, what are we going to do? You and me?' she asked eventually, kissing his face and allowing her fingers to explore his bare body.

'When, now? Or for ever?' He responded to her touch and clung to her with all his strength, crushing her slender body to his.

'Jack! That hurts – you're too strong!'

'I'm never going to let you go,' he said. 'Never. So that answers your question!'

'And will you be seeing me at Christmas?' she asked, easing herself out of his tight grip.

'Yes, of course.'

'I mean on Christmas Day,' she said slowly. 'I want to cook Christmas dinner, Jack, just for you and me. Will you be able to come? I don't want to spend Christmas all alone. I would like you to come, Jack, to be with me the whole day.'

'I can't leave Emmerdale on Christmas Day,' he said. 'I've always had my Christmas dinner there, with Ma and the family. Even Joe's coming, all the way from France to be there. It's a big family occasion, Karen. Everybody comes.'

'So what about another day – just one day out of the holiday for me? Surely you can find some reason to get away.'

'That's not going to be easy . . .'

'Nobody says it will be easy, Jack. They'll all have each other, won't they? Pat'll have Sandie and

43

Jackie and she must have suspected about you by now . . . she'll be glad to have you out of the way, surely?'

'I don't know, Karen . . .' He was hesitating now.

'Please, Jack,' and she kissed him passionately this time, her hands caressing him more urgently, exciting him as only she could. 'Give me a happy Christmas, Jack, the happiest I could ever wish for.'

Chapter Three

Joe's presence at Emmerdale that Christmas brought moments of joy where there would have been over-whelming gloom and despondency. He had arrived late on Christmas Eve with his arms full of colourful boxes of presents from France, to place among the others piled around the decorated tree in the par-lour. Having slept late at Demdyke Cottage, he came to join the family at the farm on Christmas morning. Jackie *was* going to the Caswells' house for dinner, but everyone else would be there – including Jack.

Everyone was busy when Joe arrived. Jack and Jackie were outside, finishing the milking and clean-ing out the mistle before the festivities started, and Joe wandered into the kitchen, where he found the women in the throes of producing Christmas dinner. There wasn't a spare inch of space in the kitchen, and the heat almost knocked him out.

'How about a cup of coffee, Ma?' Joe tried to find someone to talk to.

'If you want one you'll have to make it yourself!' grinned Annie. 'And while you're at it, we could all do with one. Then you can light the fire in the parlour. Grandad's Yule log will be somewhere, you'll have to look for it, it's probably in his shed. I don't want his old custom to die out . . . Then there's the drinks to see to . . .'

The morning vanished in a haze of activity and then it was time to open the presents. Jack and Jackie had finished their morning's work and changed into clean clothes, while the goose was in the oven and the dinner underway under Annie's skilled directions. As was the practice, the entire family, including Matt, Dolly and little Sam, went into the parlour to open their presents before eating. The fire was blazing with logs from the farm and Joe had found Grandad's Yule log; it was smouldering too. It would be entirely consumed this year, and a new log would take its place. This would be partially burnt with flames from the old log, then kept for next year.

They received and gave their presents, with enthusiasm, with young Sam rifling the heap of boxes for anything that might be for him. Among the presents Joe had brought was a selection of little clay figures from Aubagne in France, one for every member of his family.

'They're called *santons*,' he said. 'It means "little saints", and French families use them to make cribs in their homes, little collections of happy families. You can get all kinds now – musicians, poachers, animals and other figures, in addition to biblical characters.'

But somehow the distribution of presents, coupled with Joe's effervescent cheeriness and chatter did not entirely lift the unhappiness that permeated Emmerdale Farm this Christmas holiday.

When Jackie left for his visit to the Caswells, Joe caught his mother brushing a tear from her eyes. She had gone into the kitchen ostensibly to check the

46

progress of the dinner, but Joe realised she had wanted to be alone.

'All right, Ma?' he asked sympathetically.

'Aye, just missing Dad.' She put on a brave smile. 'It's not the same without him, is it? He loved Christmas, you know, Midnight Mass, and all the carols, the family traditions and colours in the decorations and lights, the trees and presents – we've got to keep it the way he would have liked it, Joe.'

'We will, Ma,' he reassured her. 'We will.'

'Funnily enough, I wish Jackie had been here, somehow it's not the same with both him and Dad absent, not a family occasion any more. But I'm so glad you came, I really am. Sandie's gloomy too, worrying about her dad spending Christmas in prison – I'm trying not to be miserable, Joe, but I find it so hard to be cheerful amongst it all. It would have been a real misery without you, it really would.'

'Summat wrong between Pat and Jack, is there?' Joe asked her quietly.

'You've noticed?' Annie put to him.

'Anybody can see things aren't right,' Joe told her. 'When Pat gave him that lovely sweater, he never even kissed her, and he looked bored to tears as he gave her that gold necklace; it was almost as if he was thinking of somebody else.'

Annie sighed.

'Mebbe you could have a word with him, Joe, sometime when you feel the moment's right. I don't know what's got into our Jack lately, he's certainly not himself. But he won't tell anybody what's troubling him.'

'He allus was a deep 'un,' acknowledged Joe.

47

'Call them all in for dinner, will you?' Annie asked. 'It's ready now. We can sit down.'

And so with Annie appearing happy, the family settled down to her goose and all the tasty trimmings of an Emmerdale Christmas dinner. Annie's eyes were on Jack.

'Aren't you hungry, Jack? You've hardly touched that goose!'

'Sorry, Ma, no, I'm not all that hungry.' But he could not tell them he'd eaten a full Christmas dinner yesterday at Karen's flat, cooked especially for him. He couldn't tell them of his wonderful afternoon when he was supposed to be Christmas shopping . . . he was thinking of her now, missing her dreadfully and wishing he could see her with her gold necklace about her beautiful throat. He'd bought an identical one for Pat too . . .

Pat also realised that Jack's mind was elsewhere. She had tried to elicit the reason from him, but he had stubbornly refused to talk to her; even so, she made a determined effort not to spoil the family Christmas with her own worries. But she was pleased when that Christmas Day ended; she looked forward to a time when she could be alone with Jack, without the eyes of the family constantly upon her.

When Christmas was over, Annie invited Pat to the Harrogate sales, but she declined, thinking that with everyone out of the house she would have an opportunity to talk things over with Jack without worry of the family intruding upon their troubles. For a time, Pat did wonder why he had not found an excuse to visit Hotten that day, but refrained from

48

aggravating the situation by asking such a direct question.

On that quiet Saturday afternoon, therefore, with the excitement of Christmas over and the unknown problems of the New Year yet to come, she made him a cup of tea and placed a scone oozing hot butter and strawberry jam on a plate. The scene was set for her chat. When she was ready, fully composed for this ordeal, she called him in from the mistle where he was doing some maintenance work on the milking machinery.

'Oh, ta,' he smiled when he saw the scone. 'All alone?'

'Yes,' she said, sitting before him. 'It's nice, isn't it, having the house to ourselves.'

'Aye,' he agreed. 'That's summat that doesn't often happen, eh?'

'I wondered,' she began hesitantly. 'I wondered, Jack, if we could talk. Now, I mean, now we're alone.'

'Talk? What about?' He bit into the scone but avoided looking into her eyes.

'About us, Jack. You and me. What's gone wrong between us, why we aren't lovers any more, why you keep vanishing from the house, going over to Hotten and so on. Jack, you must tell me the truth, you can't keep me in suspense like this.'

'Pat, I . . .'

She would not let him interrupt. 'I've been watching you, you know, and I'm not stupid . . . and this Christmas has been so nice, having you here, happy and cosy with us all . . .'

'Pat . . .' he tried again.

'No, listen. I must have my say, Jack. I know why you haven't been to Hotten over the holiday – it's because the Mart has been shut, eh? Sandie's been at home on holiday so that means your lady friend is also away on holiday, doesn't it? The office is closed. That's why you've been here all over Christmas – there was nowhere else for you to go, was there, Jack? I do know there is another woman, so don't lie to me any more, don't try to decieve me, Jack. Not now, not any more!'

'Oh, come on Pat . . .'

'Please, Jack! Don't deny it. It's no good. I *know*, Jack. Can't you see? I know there is another woman and I know who she is. And, as from now, you are not sharing my bed any more. You'll have to use the box room or Grandad's room from now on, not our room or our bed. And I want to know what you intend doing about me. Shall I leave after the holiday? Find another house? Tell me what you want me to do, Jack . . .'

All Pat's anger and anxiety poured out, and having released her fears in this confrontation with Jack, she burst into tears and ran from the kitchen. Jack sat stunned, his scone half eaten and his own mind now in a turmoil. He went upstairs to his room and sat with his head in his hands, his eyes moist with unshed tears and his heart full of the sorrow he had caused. And he knew that he could not leave Pat, the farm, this kind of life.

But he could not leave Karen either.

He spent half an hour in his room, in their room, on the bed shared so happily until so recently, and then he went for a walk up to the fells where the

50

chill winds of winter brought colour to his cheeks and made the blood surge through his veins. Although he loved Pat, he longed for Karen at this moment, he longed to talk with her, to touch her and to be with her, but she was out of reach. Her parents, in their tiny home at Richmond, did not even have a telephone, and he knew Karen would not ring Emmerdale over this holiday. So he had to wait until her office resumed work in the New Year. In the meantime, he had to cope with life at Emmerdale, to live with Pat, Ma, Joe, Jackie, Sandie – Sandie who also knew . . . and Ma? Did Ma know? Did she suspect?

'Oh, God, what a mess,' he shouted to the wind of the fells.

On a fine, frosty morning a couple of days later, Pat was hanging her washing on the line when Annie approached her.

'Pat, luv,' she smiled. 'I can't help noticing, but Jack's moved out of his bedroom, into the box room. Things not going well between you? You can always talk, you know, it doesn't do to keep things bottled up.'

'I don't want to worry you and the others with our domestic upsets, Ma. It's our problem, mine and Jack's.'

'It's our problem if the whole family feels it, luv.'

Pat sighed. 'I'm sorry, Ma, honest I am. I hoped I was keeping it from you . . .'

'Pat, I've had enough ups and downs in my marriage to realise there's times when you want to be alone.'

'I reckon I'll be spending more than a few nights on my own from now on, Ma,' Pat sounded bitter now. 'But I can't say the same for Jack.'

'Pat!' There was anguish in Annie's eyes now. 'Pat, what do you mean?'

'Your son, Annie. Haven't you noticed? All he has to do when he feels lonely is drive into Hotten where his lady friend has a bed waiting . . .'

'Pat! You can't be serious . . .'

'I am, Ma. Oh, I am,' and she burst into tears. Annie put an arm around her shoulders and walked her back into the house.

'Pat, I had no idea it was this . . .'

'I've tried to hide it, Annie, I'm sorry.' Pat dabbed her eyes with her handkerchief as she sat at the kitchen table. 'Do you think I should leave the farm? He doesn't want me any more . . . I may as well go.'

'Pat, you mustn't talk like that. Jack can't go on seeing this other woman, not even our Jack's that selfish and stupid. Somebody's got to bring him back to his senses, Pat, and . . .'

'He won't listen to me, Ma, he won't even talk to me about it, he just gets up and walks away when I try to discuss it.'

'Does Joe know? Mebbe a man-to-man talk would help.'

'I've no idea. I don't know who knows and who doesn't – I think Sandie suspects summat and Matt and Dolly as well. Jackie's too busy with his own love life,' and Pat smiled through her tears with pleasure at her son's evident happiness.

'I don't know what to say, Pat, except that I can't believe our Jack would be so stupid.'

'What can I do, Ma? Leave him, do you think? Shall I go away – do you think that would bring him to his senses?'

'No, Pat, no. You stay here, this is your home. Always remember that. You musn't give him up as easily as that – that's if you still love him . . .'

'Oh, yes, I do,' she cried.

'Then you must fight for him, Pat. Fight with everything in your power. And never give in and never even hint of leaving Emmerdale, right?'

'Thanks, Ma, it's nice having a family, isn't it?'

'Aye – sometimes!' grinned Annie. 'Come on, there's work to be done.'

Pat's talk with Annie lifted her spirits immensely. Now that she was able to share her problem, it seemed there was hope where only days ago there had been none. With renewed faith and determination, she busied herself with the rest of the washing, hanging it out to dry in the bright winter sunshine and then returning to the ironing-board to complete that which was already dry. She was even humming to herself as she worked, a sign which brought a smile to Annie's face. She left Pat to her chores knowing she'd want a few moments to herself, saying she was popping down the village to see the vicar about the January and February flower rotas for the church.

At tea-time, Jack came in, thirsty after a long afternoon of cleaning out the cattle food store and the implement shed, two tasks that were long overdue.

'Tea?' Pat broke off from her ironing and smiled

briefly at her husband. It was a smile with no warmth.

'Aye, thanks,' and he went to the sink to wash his hands.

Pat made the tea and found an almond tart in the cake tin which she placed on a plate for him. Then she waited until he sat down and joined him.

'Jack,' she made a firm effort to be calm. 'When are you seeing Karen again?'

He shrugged his shoulders. 'No idea . . .'

'She'll be back at work next Monday, won't she? After the New Year break. Like Sandie.'

'I suppose so, she hasn't said.'

'What are you going to tell her, Jack? I'm not leaving here, by the way, so you've got to make a choice; it's either me and the family, or it's Karen. It's that simple.'

'It's not that simple,' he almost shouted. 'God, I wish it was . . . Pat . . . you just don't know.'

'Jack, I know what love means; I know I love you in spite of everything, and I want you here at my side, as my husband, for today and for ever. It's as simple as that.'

'It isn't as simple as that!' he shouted. 'And I do love you, Pat, I really do, and that's why it's so difficult. Can you love two people at once? I don't claim to know the answer. All I do know is that she loves me, she makes me feel very happy and content and I love her, Pat, I really do. And I love you as well . . . oh, God, it's so bloody hard.'

'Jack, if you persist with seeing Karen, you're going to destroy yourself and this family. And her too. You can't continue like this. You've got to make a choice. The minute she gets back you must go and see her and tell her it's all over. That's the only way, Jack – for all our sakes.'

'Yes,' he said softly. 'Yes, it is. Pat, dearest Pat, I know I've been rotten to you, but I do love you, I really do, and these past months have been hell on earth, they really have.'

She went across to him and kissed him. 'Then come to your senses and tell her it's over, Jack. There's a new year coming and a chance for a new start for us all if this affair is stopped, so just tell her that.'

'Aye,' he said softly. 'I will.'

Jack had never discussed his problem with anyone except Karen and Pat; he had considered a visit to the vicar, not for spiritual advice, but for a man-to-man talk, but had rejected this because he felt Hinton's views would be based too firmly within those of the Church. He'd thought of Henry Wilks too, but Henry had gone to Italy to visit his daughter Marian over the Christmas break. And Matt? He'd considered a long chat with Matt, but felt he'd be too biased, too close to the other members of the family, too influenced by Dolly, even. But Joe was here, and Joe was good at looking at problems objectively.

The following morning, New Year's Eve, Joe decided to help Jack clean the mistle and they began to swill away the muck. As they worked, Joe was chattering about his work in France, saying how he was struggling against the bureaucracy of NY Estates in his efforts to modernise the farming equipment on their French estates.

'You wouldn't believe it, Jack, their stuff is ancient – and I mean ancient, not just old! But the minute I start wanting things, Head Office, which is hundreds of miles away in England, gives me a thousand reasons why I shouldn't have them! They talk about money and priorities and setting precedents and I spend my time answering daft questions instead of getting on with the job.'

'You'd be better off here, Joe, working for yourself.'

'There's times I think I would, Jack. I do miss this, you know; it's nice to be back like this, helping out again and getting my hands mucky instead of coping with mountains of paperwork.'

'That's the penalty of having a secure, pensioned job, Joe. Don't you fancy working for yourself again? Having the freedom to stand by your own decisions?'

'Yes, of course I do. But I'm learning fast through my work, Jack. Learning how to run a big business, how to raise capital, how to cope with EEC rules and regulations – it's a big job, Jack, and I aim to rise further.'

'I wish you every luck then, if that's what you want.'

'How about you and me having a long talk over a pint later?' Joe said. 'It's New Year's Eve, you and Pat don't want to stay in and be miserable.'

'No, I think I'll see the New Year in at home, thanks.'

Joe halted his work and studied his brother. 'Jack, what's up between you and Pat? A blind man could see things aren't well between you. I reckon it's time you tackled it, whatever it is, and got yourself sorted out. I'm only visiting but I can sense the tension, so God knows what Ma and the rest of them feel like.'

Jack did not respond for several minutes, swilling the floor of the mistle as he brooded over Joe's comments. Then he said, 'I'd welcome a chat, Joe. But not in the pub. How about Demdyke?'

'Aye, right. Jackie's out tonight, isn't he? He's going to a New Year party at Connelton with Alison, so we won't be seeing him until next year!'

'Half-eight then?' suggested Jack. 'The two of us.'

'Done,' said Joe. For Joe, this would be one of those rare occasions when he and Jack confided in each other. Ma had been right. Jack was having problems and he did need somebody, a man, to talk to. Joe was pleased Ma had suggested this idea.

When Jack arrived that evening, Joe had some drinks ready and had made a plate of ham sand-wiches, complemented by the remains of a Christ-mas cake and some mince pies. Joe poured Jack a beer and then one for himself and they settled down.

Jack took the initiative.

'You've noticed things haven't been well with me and Pat.' He made a determined effort to go straight into the subject. 'Is it that obvious?'

'Aye, it is, Jack, and as I said, anybody can see it. So what's the problem? Marriages do go through rough patches – all of 'em. And I should know!'

'It's more than that, Joe. I'm seeing someone else, another woman.'

'Oh,' and Joe sipped his beer, this revelation now

57

explaining a great deal. 'So how long's this been going on?'

'Months now, five or six, more mebbe. I kept it quiet, Joe; in fact, I never thought it would get to this stage. You know how it is – you find somebody attractive, you talk, then you meet for drinks, then a meal . . . and well, the next thing you know is you're head-over-heels in love. And I do love her, Joe, and she loves me. It's not just an infatuation.'

'You've not seen her over Christmas?'

'No, she's been at home with her parents; she is single, by the way.'

'And Pat knows?'

'Aye. I think she's suspected for a long time, but she never said a word till Christmas was over. She wants me to ditch the other woman, Joe. I don't know what to do.'

'And you love Pat? You couldn't bear it if she left you and went away from Emmerdale?'

'Right. I do love her – and I love the other one.'

'Who else knows? Ma knows summat is wrong, but she didn't explain what it was.'

'Dolly, Matt, Sandie, Ma – they all know. All except Jackie – he's too busy with his own love life.'

'So what do you want me to say, Jack? You've never been one for listening to me, have you?'

'I know you can't give advice and I know I'd probably ignore it anyway, but I just wanted to tell somebody about it.'

'That does help sometimes,' added Joe.

'I've needed to have somebody to explain to them how I feel, what a berk I am, to get it off my chest, to open it up.'

'Right, well, I'm all ears, Jack. It's hardly a secret any more, is it?'

'No,' and Jack sipped at his drink. 'Well, thanks for giving me your time. Now, I first met her when I went to Hotten Mart . . .'

And so Jack poured out his story, for the first time telling someone about his months with Karen. Joe was a good and patient listener and Jack felt better for the chat, even if it did not immediately solve anything. They both knew that Joe could never find a solution to this dilemma – only Jack could do that.

'The thing is, Jack,' said Joe eventually, 'you have a fine wife, you have a good home and you have a family right here. On top of that, you've got the family farm and an inheritance for your family, Jackie, I mean. Are you going to chuck it all away? All that – and for what? If you give up Pat you could find yourself living in a grotty bed-sit somewhere in blackest Hotten with nobody to love you and no future, because this woman might ditch you when she'd had enough of you and your moods. You're not the first man who's ever fancied another woman, you know – and you'll not be the last. But it's up to you, Jack. Only you can stop this madness – because it is daft, and you know it.'

'You make it sound so bloody simple; it's not simple, Joe. I can't just stop loving her like that . . . just give it all up . . .'

'If you don't, you'll finish up with nobody -- Jack, you know what to do. So go and do it. Before you make it any worse.'

'Aye,' said Jack. 'I will. And a Happy New Year to you!' he added with more than a hint of bitterness.

* * *

The arrival of that New Year was not the happiest of events at Emmerdale Farm, least of all for Jack, who now appreciated the effect his affair was having upon everyone else. Jackie was the only exception – he still seemed oblivious to the strained atmosphere and his mother's unhappiness.

Sandie was one who had a double reason to be critical of Jack.

'I'm not looking forward to starting work again,' she said to Pat. 'It means working with Karen, sharing an office. She was my best friend, she is my work colleague . . .'

'You'll be busy, luv.' Pat smiled at her with sympathy. 'I can cope now, you'll see.'

'But Jack will be hanging about, wanting to see her. I know what all this is doing to you, Mum, and think you've coped wonderfully, but I wish I could do something to stop it. Karen is a nice girl – er, was a nice girl.'

'It's all in the open now, Sandie, and that's a marvellous tonic for me.'

'But it isn't over, is it?'

'Jack's going to see Karen – to end it all. He said he would.'

Sandie just looked at her mother as if to say, You don't believe that, do you?

Pat recognised her reaction and countered it with, 'He is, Sandie.'

'Then I hope he doesn't hang about. He should make the break today or as soon as he can.'

'He will, luv.'

'Mum, I don't know how you coped with this over

60

Christmas. Trying to be normal, making us feel happy and so on.'

'Oh, I've cried, Sandie, many times. I've been out in the buildings weeping bucketsful of tears over the calves, or letting the wind on the fells blow them away. I've cried, believe me, but mostly where Jack could not see me. I must appear to be in control even if there's times I'm not so sure.'

'He will end it all, won't he?' Sandie asked.

'He will,' said Pat with a confidence Sandie wished she could share.

Jack telephoned Karen at the office soon after ten o'clock that Monday morning; she was busy with a couple of customers and could not talk to him, although she did agree to see him just as soon as possible. He said he could come to her flat that evening, if it was all right with her. She said it was.

He arrived at eight o'clock bearing a bottle of wine and a bouquet of flowers; she had just climbed out of the bath, and was draped in a large, soft towel which gaped to reveal her slender legs as she walked across the room, filling the air with the scent of her bath oil. She looked stunning; her skin was clean and pink and her eyes sparkled with happiness. He felt a surge of desire as he admired her beauty, hardly daring to believe that such a wonderful woman could find him attractive.

'Sorry to be so long,' she apologised. 'Did you find something to drink?'

'Yes, thanks. I poured one for you, it's there when you're ready,' and as she dried her hair, he put on a tape of Barbara Dickson songs. He listened to the

61

music, drank his wine and occasionally caught glimpses of Karen's lithe body as she changed into a loose-fitting dress and slippers.

'What shall we do tonight?' she asked as she settled beside him on the settee.

'I'm happy staying in,' he said. 'Just being with you – it has been a long Christmas without you,' he added, kissing her and holding her tight.

'I missed you,' she told him. 'No phone calls even; I went into Richmond several times and picked up the phone in a kiosk, but decided I daren't ring you, not over the holiday.'

'That was considerate of you. I had a tough time, wanting you but being with the family. Did you think I wouldn't come back to see you?' he asked.

'I must admit I wondered; I mean, you being at home, in the bosom of your family, as they say, I thought you might decide that it was all over between you and me, that you'd want to end it before we got any more serious.'

'Karen!'

'Jack, I know the dangers. I'm not stupid, you know.'

'Well, seeing you've brought that up, there is something we'd better talk over, Karen . . .'

'Not a discussion about fidelity, love, marriage and family life, Jack. Not tonight.'

'But, seriously, Karen, there are things to talk about, things to discuss, to decide on . . .'

She put a finger across his lips to silence him and said, 'Yes, but not tonight. Tonight, I want to be happy. I've not seen you for nearly two weeks and I want to make up for lost time, Jack. I want you to make love to me tonight, now.'

And she rose from the settee, took his hand and led him towards her bedroom.

Chapter Four

The Home Farm office of NY Estates was a very busy place during the early weeks of the new year. Caroline Bates, Alan Turner's secretary, returned to work after the break to find a massive heap of unopened letters on her desk. In addition, there was a note on top of the pile saying Mr Turner had been called away to a meeting in Skipdale, and that he expected to be back after lunch. He asked her to deal with the mail and to respond to any routine letters.

With a sigh of resignation, she made herself a cup of coffee and settled down with her letter opener to tackle the mass of envelopes. One by one, she slit them open, discarding all the circulars without bothering to read them; they rapidly filled the wastepaper basket beside her desk. Once she got into a rhythm, the chore became easier.

Eventually, she had a much reduced pile of correspondence. Some, she knew, would be easy to cope with herself, requiring merely an acknowledgment or a fairly standard reply. Others, memos from Head Office or letters which required Mr Turner's personal attention, she placed in a separate pile for transference to his 'In' tray.

By mid-morning, she felt she had overcome those awful 'return to work blues', and was cheerfully dealing with the routine replies when Seth Armstrong came in.

'Morning, Mrs Bates, had a good holiday?'

'Very pleasant, Seth. And you?'

'Aye, very nice. I managed to keep out of our Meg's road, which meant she couldn't shout at me, and I got a pint or two as well. Anyroad, it's the boss I'm after.'

'He's out, Seth, till this afternoon. Anything I can do?'

'It's about the staff outing, Mrs Bates. He said summat about organising a trip to Scarborough or Bridlington for the work force. Well, me and the lads have had a chat about it and it's not really the time for going to the seaside, is it? So we thought we'd like to go to Cleethorpes instead.'

'But that's a seaside town, Seth!' she pointed out.

'Is it? I've heard you can't see the sea at Cleethorpes, but I have heard tell there's some good clubs there with high-class acts, and they say there's a big posh indoor entertainment centre with snooker, darts and so on. Nice chip shops, an' all, and it's not too far from here, give or take an hour or two. We've been to Scarborough before, Mrs Bates, and to Bridlington an' all, so we'd like to go to Cleethorpes this time. Tell Mr Turner it's the overwhelming decision of the work force, and if you'd tell him about it, we'd be very pleased. I've seen about a bus, tell him an' all; they can fit us in, and we're not too bothered about the date, so long as it's in the next month or two on a Saturday afternoon.'

'As you wish, Seth.'

And off went Seth, moustache bristling with satisfaction at the outcome of his visit.

The staff outing must have been discussed without her knowledge, but she made a note to inform Alan Turner. Caroline guessed that Seth had some devious scheme in mind and an ulterior motive for insisting on Cleethorpes for an outing. Was there a particularly good club there? Or a spectacular variety show? But that was Alan Turner's problem, not hers, and she returned to her pile of unanswered mail.

As she dealt with each letter, she came upon a sheaf of papers that bore an air of officialdom. She began to read what, with a shock, she realised was some very private correspondence – papers relating to his divorce from Mrs Gillian Turner. It was the first Caroline had known of the matter. Hurriedly, she sought the envelope, hoping to reseal the package and hide the fact she had opened it. But it was no good – she did find the envelope, but it had been torn in the process, and there was no way she could cover up her mistake. She would have to tell him of her error – in cases like this, honesty was always the best policy – and so she placed the file in a new envelope and sealed it to protect the contents from other prying eyes.

Before resuming work, she felt a touch of sympathy for Turner, especially because, over Christmas, she and her husband had not been happy either. She had caught him talking conspiratorially on the telephone and had overheard the name Sonia. This confirmed her earlier suspicions and now she knew that Malcolm was meeting someone else.

There had been a terrible row, and talk of a separation with Caroline stressing her wish to have custody of their teenage children, Nick and Kathy. What was wrong with the world, she asked herself, with so many insecure marriages?

When Alan Turner came back he was in a benevolent mood, having had lunch with some country landowners who had not spared their hospitality in their efforts to secure some cut-price shooting days on NY's well-stocked land.

As he poured himself a cup of coffee, he said, 'You know, Mrs Bates, though I do say it myself, I have driven a hard bargain today. I'm sure I impressed my guests with the facilities we can offer and, of course, they said they would include me in any of their parties, both here and away from NY Estates. Very reasonable fellows, Mrs Bates; men of quality, I would add,' and she knew he also saw himself in that light.

He settled at his desk and began to examine the heap of mail in his 'In' tray, sifting through quickly, nodding to himself as he made snap decisions.

'Er, Mr Turner, there is something I must mention,' Caroline said tentatively.

'Yes, of course, Mrs Bates. It is important? I do have to plough through this lot before I leave and I am having dinner with Colonel J. R. Pemberton tonight, at the Feathers, you know. He's a very influential member of the County Council and . . .'

'Yes, it is important. Very.' And she withdrew the heavy envelope from her desk drawer. 'It's this,' And she carried it over to him.

'By hand, eh?' He noticed it bore no stamps.

'Not exactly,' she said. 'Mr Turner, in the rush this morning, I opened one of your personal letters by mistake. I put it in here, for confidentiality. I read part of it before I realised it was a very private one, you see, and just wanted to apologise . . .'

'Oh, well, these things do happen, Mrs Bates. I know that whatever you read will be treated with the strictest of confidence . . . but I know of nothing that's so secret it has to be wrapped up like this.' He tore open the envelope, then said, 'Ah, well, yes. Nasty . . .'

'I'm sorry, Mr Turner. I had no idea what you were going through.'

'No, well, divorce is a very distasteful thing, Mrs Bates, and I hope you are never subjected to it. This looks like the final step, eh? Gillian has divorced me, but there remains the question of the final settlement over the house and contents. Perhaps it's a good thing the children are growing up.'

'Yes, I suppose so . . .'

But he was continuing, 'Terence is still at university of course, Oxford you know, but he'll soon be finished . . . and Amanda's in her final year at school, doing 'A' levels. A private education of course, a very good school. One must do one's best for one's children. Well, I suppose that's it. I don't know whether to celebrate or commiserate with myself.'

'You kept it very quiet,' she said, for want of something to say. 'No one ever knew; no one here, I mean.'

'No, well, one has to strive to separate one's private life from one's professional role, Mrs Bates, especially when one holds a position of distinction in the community. I can't say I am sorry, for Gill has had her own business – a very successful fashion retail outlet – for some time now, and we have led very separate lives for a long period. There is no other man in her life, by the way, it's just her career. She wants to be settled in one place to further her business aims, while my career with NY is liable to take me anywhere in the United Kingdom or even to the Continent. We're friends, of course, and always will be. But, you know, Mrs Bates, I'm not sure how I should react to the end of our marriage. Are racks of dresses and nighties more important than I, Mrs Bates?' and he smiled.

Suddenly, she had a new respect for her boss; she knew some men who would have burdened their secretaries and friends with endless tales of their marriage problems.

But Alan Turner had never mentioned his, not even to her. That lifted him in her esteem immensely. For all his faults, he was not a complainer, not a misery.

'You know, Mrs Bates,' he went on, 'in some ways I'm glad you opened that letter. It's brought my divorce out in the open and that means I need no longer keep up any pretence. I can talk openly about it, about Gill and me.'

'I won't breathe a word to anyone,' she promised.

'I don't mind if you do mention it, Mrs Bates. In fact, it might be an idea if you did tell a few souls – like Amos; then the whole village will get to know without me having to say anything.'

'Well, if you like . . .'

'Yes, yes, I think that would be a good idea. So here we are, me a divorced man and you happily married with a growing family. You know, Mrs Bates, I envy you – and others in this community. Look at Jack Sugden for instance – I mean, he more or less rescued Pat from that awful Tom Merrick, married her and has lived happily ever since with his own farm into the bargain. He's a very fortunate man, Mrs Bates, and here am I, a leader of this community, now divorced, and living in someone else's house while working for something as impersonal as NY Estates . . . Really, I have nothing, Mrs Bates. Nothing.'

She felt tempted to talk to him about her own worries, about Malcolm's infidelity, but decided that this was not the time. Instead she said, 'Oh, there is another thing, Mr Turner. Seth came in about the staff outing.'

'Yes, they were on about going to a nightclub in Scarborough or Bridlington, an early spring trip of some kind.'

'I haven't been told a thing about it yet and I'm staff too,' she smiled. 'But Seth says the men want to go to Cleethorpes.'

'Cleethorpes?' he burst out. 'What on earth is there at Cleethorpes? I'll have a word with him about that!'

'They seem fairly set on the idea,' she said.

'If Seth Armstrong's behind this, there'll be some devious plot afoot,' he grinned. 'But the outing is for everyone, you understand, husbands, wives, girlfriends, that sort of thing. Why don't you come, and bring your husband along? And the children, of course. Do a memo to the work force to remind them to ask their families.'

'Yes, I will, but I think I'll see what Seth has planned first,' she smiled.

'A very wise idea,' he agreed.

Someone else whose relationship with the opposite sex was not progressing too smoothly was Jackie Merrick. With the euphoria of Christmas and New Year over, he was settling down again to helping run Emmerdale Farm where he was rapidly acquiring the skills of shepherding from Matt Skilbeck.

He was discovering the satisfaction of working with animals, and felt he had the makings of a shepherd or a sheep farmer. Alison was a big help in this; whenever she could get time away from her parents' farm, she came to Emmerdale to assist Jackie, especially if he was working late or at weekends.

On one occasion, half a dozen Emmerdale ewes had become separated from the main flock. In spite of long searches by everyone, including Jackie and Alison, the ewes were still missing a couple of days later. Matt even considered informing the police in case they had been stolen. It was Alison who eventually discovered the ewes, huddled on the side of Pencross Fell. Somehow, they had scrambled through a broken section of a drystone wall and strayed almost a mile from the farm. But she spotted them and drove them back to safety.

It was actions like this that had made the mouse-like but determined girl so much a part of Emmerdale Farm. In fact, she was increasingly regarded as one of the family and she and Jackie seemed almost inseparable. Wherever one of them went, the other would not be far behind. Out shopping, going to the Mart, visiting friends, working with the sheep, cleaning the mistle, servicing the tractor, and even cleaning out Demdyke Cottage, or milking at dawn, Alison was constantly at Jackie's side.

Whenever a family matter was discussed or plans were made, Alison Caswell was included with Jackie. They were partners now, and was it generally expected that it would not be long before they were man and wife. Everyone at Emmerdale, and many in Beckindale, too, agreed that Alison and Jackie were ideal for one another and that this union, with its consequent links between Emmerdale Farm and Caswell's holding at Fellside Farm, would be highly beneficial to all concerned.

Jackie was saving hard; instead of spending money on the motor bike of his dreams, he tolerated his old machine with all its faults and invested in a building society.

While working with Matt, he discussed his marriage ideas, talked of a honeymoon grape-picking in France and of buying a cottage of their very own, one that was in need of some repair so that he and Alison could fashion it to their own ideas and inject it with their own character.

Eventually, as if to give formal recognition to the relationship, Annie invited Alison's parents to tea at Emmerdale Farm. She had known Janet and Frank Caswell for years and although they were not close friends of the folks at Emmerdale, they had always all got on well together.

However, it was around this time that Jackie realized his feelings for Alison were undergoing a change.

Frank Caswell's behaviour at the tea party added to his growing belief that he and Alison would not marry. Jackie had watched the fellow behave like a glutton, eating everything that was on the table, filling himself with left-overs, cleaning out the dishes, polishing off the cakes, and all the time chortling over his mammoth appetite. Jackie found that he now minded more about this than he had at Christmas and did not relish the idea of having this man as a father-in-law; not only was he greedy, but he was also uncouth, and from the mouselike behaviour of Mrs Caswell, it seemed he might also be something of a bully.

In Jackie's mind this last went some way to explain Alison's limpet-like behaviour. She would never leave Jackie alone, she was always at his side. This was a sign of her love for him, yes, but Jackie also saw it as a symptom of subservience – he imagined Mrs Caswell would have been just like that with her husband.

It was Jackie's increasing desire for a little time without Alison occasionally, that began to unsettle him. When he told her he wanted to go out without her she never made any fuss but just turned up unannounced, even at his all-male gatherings. There was the example of the party at Demdyke, when Jackie invited Archie Brooks, Mike West and a few others round for a music and drinking session. It was an occasion likely to become a wild party – and all male. But Alison had turned up uninvited at half-past ten – her excuse was that she would tidy up afterwards.

'You do love me, Jackie?' she'd said when the lads had all gone home.

'Yeh, yeh, course I do.' He'd helped her to clean up the glasses and empty the ashtrays.

'You didn't want me to come here, though, did you?' she'd put to him.

'It was a booze-up for the lads, that's all,' he'd tried to explain. 'Me, Archie and a few more. Just having a sing-song and a few drinks, nowt else. No other women, Alison, it's nowt to do with not loving you. Lads like to have fun, that's all.'

'I thought you'd always want me at your side,' she'd said with unhappiness in her voice.

Jackie had tried to explain that the fact he wanted to meet his pals from time to time, without her, was not an indication of any desire to end their romance.

'I do love you, Alison, I really do, but haven't you some other friends, some girls, to go out with? You know, to the cinema, to parties or just shopping in Harrogate, that kind of thing?'

'No, there's just you,' she'd told him sincerely.

It was that remark that made Jackie wonder if Alison would begin to become a burden rather than an asset to him.

One dark January evening, Pat discovered Jack in her bedroom. He was seeking his best suit and hunting through his wardrobe for a smart tie and some cufflinks.

'Going out?' she asked, knowing the answer.

'Yes,' was his short response.

'You were going to end it, Jack, you promised.'

'That's why I'm going out, to talk to her, to tell her it's all over.'

'You had your chance last time, why didn't you tell her then? Did she get you into bed with tales of exotic plans and other such feminine wiles, eh?'

'No,' he lied. Karen *had* got him into bed, and though he had tried to call off the whole affair, she hadn't allowed it to happen . . . he just hadn't had the courage to tell her straight out.

'You don't want to end it, do you?' Pat continued the onslaught. 'You've got me at home to do your washing, and her in Hotten to minister to your more personal needs . . .'

'Pat, it's not like that! I've got to talk to her, I can't just ring up and say there's no more.'

'You can! Why can't you do that? Why string her along – and me as well? Jack, you're behaving like a bastard, you really are.'

He stormed out of the room and went to the bathroom to change, leaving his working clothes in the box room where he was still having to sleep. Feeling the bastard that Pat said he was, he went downstairs in his smart suit.

In the kitchen, Annie, Pat, Matt, Sandie and Dolly were seated around the table, with young Sam playing on the floor. As Jack entered the room, they all ceased talking and watched in silence as he walked towards the door in a cloud of aftershave. No one said a word as he left, not even 'goodbye'.

Then Annie looked at Pat. 'Pat, luv, I am sorry.'

It was Sandie who cried out, 'Mum, you can't just let him go like this, you've got to do something . . .'

'He's going to finish it tonight; he said he would.' Then Pat burst into tears and ran upstairs.

'Leave her,' said Annie as Dolly and Sandie prepared to go after her. 'She'll be best on her own.'

There followed a long silence, and then Matt said, 'Ma, somebody's got to knock some sense into Jack.'

'Pat's working on that, Matt; she knows what he's up to and who it is, and she is going to sort it all out.'

'It needs stopping, Ma, quite apart from Pat's feelings. I mean, suppose Jack leaves, or Pat for that matter? What'll happen to the farm? To us, me, Dolly and little Sam? To Ma? Jackie? There's a lot of mouths feeding from Emmerdale's income and we can't all sit back and let Jack destroy us. It belongs to us all, Ma, not just Jack.'

'They are talking about it, Matt; Pat knows everything. She's in a determined mood and she's going to fight to keep Jack. I know she'll sort it out. And if Jack goes, we'll manage without him – we've managed before, when he was in Rome.'

'Aye, but Joe was here then, don't forget.'

'And now we've got Jackie to help,' Annie countered. 'Matt, we'll cope, you'll see, if the worst comes to the worst. But I've told Pat this is her home, and that she hasn't to even think of leaving. But I reckon it'll not come to that.'

'I wish I had your confidence, Ma. Jack can be as stubborn as they come, you know, and right now he's besotted with that woman. His work's suffering because he's going round in a dream and he's not even thinking straight.'

'Give it time, Matt; it's only just come into the open, and time's a marvellous healer.'

Matt said nothing more except, 'Come on, Dolly. Fetch Sam and we'll go home. I'll just check the top field before tea, there's a few ewes up there that need fetching down.'

Jack was seated on the edge of Karen's settee, a distance between them. 'I thought we'd eat out tonight,' he suggested.

'You've always wanted to stay in before,' she smiled. 'So what's caused this change of heart?'

'Nowt, I just wanted to buy you a good meal,' he said, not very convincingly. 'To save you having to cook. Then we can come back here.'

'All right.' Karen came closer and hugged him. 'Let's do that. I don't feel like cooking anyway.'

'And I'm useless in the kitchen.' He suddenly smiled.

'But very good in other parts of the house!' She went to the bedroom for her coat. 'Like the bedroom . . .'

'Flattery will get you everywhere,' he joked. 'We'll see about that when I return!'

Jack did buy Karen a fine meal at a new restaurant in Harrogate; it was one of the best they'd enjoyed, and afterwards, they returned to Karen's flat. She made coffee, changed into a housecoat and settled at his side on the sofa.

'Jack, you've altered,' she observed. 'You're different somehow, not cheerful like you used to be. Is something wrong?'

'It's Pat,' he said. 'She knows, Karen. They all know. My whole family . . . tonight, as I walked out, I felt like an intruder in my own house. They were all sitting around the table, and watched in total silence as I came out to meet you. God knows what they must be thinking of me now.'

She did not reply, but watched him closely, knowing the tension he felt at this moment. It showed on his face.

'I thought you sounded a bit down, remote even, when you rang. Have you told Pat, then? That you're leaving her? We can live here, Jack, and I'm sure you could get work somewhere until the farm issue has been settled . . . In the meantime, I'm on a good salary, so we wouldn't starve.'

'Karen, don't, luv. I can't even think that far ahead just now. My brain's like a whirlwind, I don't honestly know what I'm doing, why I'm doing it . . . I just don't know what's going to happen between us, all of us. You and me. Pat and me.'

'You do love me, don't you?' she said, standing before him to demand a reply. 'I mean, Jack, throughout this you've always said you loved me, and that I was special.'

'Yes, yes, and it's true. I have always loved you, Karen . . .'

'Then there's no problem, is there? You love me and I love you. That means we want to be together, now and forever.'

'I wish it was as simple as that, Karen. God, this is an awful mess.'

'You want to end it all, don't you?' she said after a moment's reflection. 'That's why you came as you did, done up in your best suit, so formal and serious. You came with the intention of taking me out of here, away from my own place, because you want to throw me aside, like a piece of used rag. You've come here to tell me that, haven't you? I should have known! That's why we went out for a meal, so you could gather your wits, so you had time to work out what to say to me.'

'I don't want to end it all, Karen. I ache for you, I've ached for you night after night when I've been away from you. But I have responsibilities . . .'

'I knew, Jack. All along I knew you'd never leave your family for me. I suppose I've been preparing for this day, for this speech. You are saying it's all over, aren't you?'

'I'm saying it's not as easy as I thought. I need time, Karen, space. I need time to make up my mind what to do, to find a way of, well, seeing you . . .'

'While living at Emmerdale with Pat, eh? You want it both ways, Jack. You want the cosy life you've created at home with your dirty socks washed and your dinner on the table, and here you want the excitement that a mistress can bring. Sex and fun with no responsibilities. Just a willing woman on hand whenever you feel like using her body . . .'

'You make it sound so crude and vulgar, Karen.'

'It is crude and vulgar if you've been using me like that,' she said. 'Look, Jack. I have made love to you and I have loved you over these last months, and I did so fully aware that you are married and that you were likely to remain so. I'm no fool, Jack; I knew I could not keep you easily . . . that is the pain I must endure. If you ask me if I've enjoyed these months, then the answer is "yes"; if you ask me if I would do it all again, then the answer is "yes". If you ask me if I ever expected our relationship to be full and permanent, with wedding bells at the end of it, then the answer must be "no", but I did hope for more than this, more than, well, just nothing. You could have lived with me, shared my life . . .'

'Karen, I do love you . . .'

'I'm sure you do, Jack. But we need more than love – and I want to know if yours was love rather than lust. I've been very available for you, Jack; your wife will think I'm a slut and a loose woman. That's the reputation I will have earned myself because of my love for you, not only with Pat but with the people of this town who've seen what's been going on. And with Sandie, of course, my friend, the daughter of your own wife, remember?'

'Karen, I'm sorry. Look, let's forget all this, let's enjoy ourselves like we have in the past. Let's give ourselves more time . . .'

'There is no more time, Jack. You have changed because your secret is now common knowledge, your little fun outings are over and it's a time of reckoning. Either you stay with me or you return to Pat. Now and for ever, Jack. It is your decision.'

'But Karen, I can't, I can't just walk out and leave you . . . or Pat for that matter. I do love you . . .'

But even as they talked, the decision was being made for them. A car eased to a halt outside Karen's flat and they heard the door slam.

'Company?' asked Jack.

'I'm not expecting anyone,' she said. 'Besides, it's a bit late for callers, isn't it?'

Jack glanced at his watch. It was almost eleven o'clock.

'It's maybe somebody coming home nearby,' she said. 'It's still the season of parties, remember.'

'And lots of happy new years with resolutions of wonderful things to come . . . I could do with a bit of New Year cheer!' he said.

But there was a visitor. Karen heard the outer door close and then footsteps on the stairs up to her flat. With a puzzled expression she turned to Jack, and then the doorbell rang. She hesitated before answering it.

'Go on, they know you're in.' He laughed uneasily.

Karen, surprisingly nervous, went to answer the door.

'Shall I hide under the bed?' Jack said. 'Maybe I'm becoming an embarrassment to you.'

'Don't be silly, Jack. I'm not expecting anyone . . .'

The bell rang again. Anxiously, she released the Yale lock and opened the door.

Pat Sugden was standing there.

'Pat!' Jack saw her at that instant and went towards her.

'I've come to take you home, Jack. Now. I'm not leaving without you.'

Jack looked at her, strangely excited by her actions, but confused. He faced Karen who stood at his side, pale-faced and almost in tears.

'Karen . . .' he said.

'Go, Jack, just go,' she said, turning away from them.

Jack didn't know which way to turn, whom to go to, but Pat simply touched his arm and said, 'Get your jacket and come with me, Jack. The car's outside.'

And she walked away, her feet clattering down the stairs as Jack went for his jacket. A blast of cool night air entered the flat as he went to kiss Karen, but she turned away.

'It's finished, Jack. Can't you see that?'

He said nothing for a long time, just looking at her, and then he heard the car engine starting up.

'Goodbye, Karen.'

She said nothing now and stood with her back towards him, covering her face and weeping into her hands. Jack wanted to touch her, to kiss her, to hold her, but he fought against these desires as the car engine ticked over outside. Then he hurried down the stairs and out into the street.

He went to the passenger door to climb in. Pat was sitting there, smiling. 'Other side, chump. This is Joe's car, it's got a left-hand drive.'

As they began the journey back to Beckindale, Jack glanced up at Karen's windows, but there was no one there.

Chapter Five.

When Joe returned to France, Annie Sudgen lapsed into a period of despondency. The farewells had not been easy, and without Joe's breezy presence about the farm, she felt Grandad's death even more acutely. It was now, as the tempo of farm work increased with the coming of spring, that she felt so much more on her own. Although Grandad had not helped much around the house, he had always been there, sitting in his favourite fireside chair or pottering about the place doing little tasks. And now he'd gone, she missed him terribly.

Jack and Pat were busy out-of-doors and she was pleased to see they were friendly again, making a firm effort to salvage their marriage. There was still a lot of tension between them, but Annie was relieved Jack was no longer visiting his woman friend. That had eased the strained atmosphere, which had permeated the farm and troubled its occupants, and things did appear to be settling down. Matt was engrossed with his sheep, more so now that lambing time was approaching, while Dolly was fully occupied with young Sam, the excitements of *The Pirates of Penzance* being over. Sandie had her job in the auctioneer's office at Hotten Mart and that kept her busy, even sometimes at weekends with auctions and winter farm sales.

Jackie's chaotic life at Demdyke Cottage, coupled

with his continuing but cooling association with Alison Caswell, meant that he was not often at the farm except when he was working. Even then, it was just a case of rushing in for meals, gulping down his food and rushing off after work to enjoy some party or outing.

And Alison continued to visit Emmerdale, sometimes alone, when she worked alongside Pat or Matt, but more often when Jackie was around. She was a nice girl, thought Annie, and she'd make a good wife for some young farmer. She wondered if Jackie would ever take that step, for in Annie's view, what had been a romance was now little more than a friendship. In some ways, she was sorry it was turning out this way.

In her loneliness, Annie took to wandering about the premises, sometimes simply spending periods of reflection in places loved by her father. There was his garden, which now awaited cultivation for the spring. Who would look after that now he'd gone? Her own rheumatism and the stiffness in her joints made it difficult to do that kind of work. So would anyone else tend his vegetable patch and make it presentable for the coming season of shows and exhibitions? And who would grow prize pumpkins, carrots, marrow and cabbages? She could hardly imagine Jack or even Jackie bothering. Then there was his shed on top of the steps, which still contained his woodwork tools and a miscellany of odds and ends. Annie had had a minor attempt at tidying up that, but had given up due to the volume of clutter it contained.

The hard and heavy work it entailed quickly

proved so painful she had ached all over, though she hoped the others would not notice these signs of her advancing age.

As she wandered about the farm and its buildings, deep in thought, she knew that her father was already nothing more than a memory. He had left this life, this home, for ever. With her eyes misting over, she realised he had never said 'Farewell'; he had simply gone away.

She knew the others missed him too, Jackie especially. One day she had climbed up to Sam's workshop to find Jackie working on something.

'Hello, Jackie,' she'd smiled, pleased to see him there. 'What's that you're doing?'

'This truck Grandad was making for young Sam,' Jackie had held the pieces for her to examine. 'He got it all cut out and shaped, as you can see. He's even made some wheels, but he never got it put together. I reckon he wanted to get it finished for Sam's birthday, but, well, it didn't work out.'

'He liked making things for young Sam,' Annie had said wistfully. 'The bairn's still playing with some bricks Dad made ages ago. Then he made him that little wooden train set – he soon had the wheels pulled off that, mind, but Dad always fixed them on again. They reckon no toy's child-proof no matter how well it's made. Now, Jackie, were you thinking of finishing that truck?'

'Aye,' Jackie had said almost shyly. 'Grandad did show me how to do things, make joints, plane the wood, prime it for painting and so on, so I thought I'd put it together. Young Sam'd like that, eh?'

'What a lovely idea, Jackie.' She had been so

pleased with him. 'Yes, you do that. And when you've finished, you and I will go through this mess, sort out his good tools from the rubbish, then mebbe you'd like to use them some more? Make other things – for yourself, I mean, your own home when you get one. Cabinets, shelves, coffee tables and so on.'

'You think I could do all that?'

She'd smiled. 'I think that's what Grandad would want you to do, lad; use your talents by making use of these tools and things. If you don't use 'em, Jackie, nobody else will.'

'Thanks, Ma, that's what I wanted to hear.'

And so Annie had returned to the kitchen feeling a little happier. Grandad had gone, but his presence was not forgotten, she realised; his quiet influence would remain for a long time at Emmerdale Farm.

Pat and Jack were together in the lowland fields, placing foodstuffs in the sheep pens. For a while they worked in silence, making sure each pen was allocated a similar amount and that the feed was spread around so that each animal could obtain its fair share. Pat knew that Jack was pre-occupied with his thoughts and decided not to interrupt him. She knew he needed time to recover from the recent drama that had disturbed his life.

Then he called across to her, 'Right, I've done this lot, so now I'll have to get up to the fells and feed the hill sheep and give 'em a check over. You coming as well?'

'I've a lot of washing to do, luv,' she said. 'You go and I'll see you later.'

'I've a gate to fix as well. A couple of spars have been smashed, somebody climbing it, I'll bet. Hikers, more than likely – some don't realise the damage they do to our walls, gates and fences.'

'Do you want me to help with the gate, then?' she offered. 'After I've got the washing done?'

He was walking towards her now, smiling with the pleasure of once again being able to communicate with his wife.

'No thanks, Pat. You see to your chores, I'll cope. I'll shout if I do need help.'

'All right.' She paused before him, happier now than she had been for many weeks. 'You were very quiet out there, Jack, when you were feeding the sheep.'

'Aye,' he smiled ruefully. 'Just thinking over how I've been behaving, not being at all proud of myself. I was thinking of you, coming over to Hotten in Joe's car to drag me away from my temptress. I'm proud of you, Pat, I really am. You made my choice for me – and I'm glad. Deep down, I'm grateful and pleased at the way you did that.'

She smiled. 'Ma said I should fight for you. It's funny, though, I didn't expect to find you sitting there chatting like you were . . .'

'I'd told her by then,' he said. 'She knew I was ending it all, and then you came. Perfect timing, really.'

'It *is* over, isn't it, Jack?' There was more than a hint of worry in Pat's voice.

'It's over,' he said. 'I'm glad, I . . . well . . . I'm sorry for what I put you through. It wasn't intended, believe me, but now you're going to have to trust me.'

'It won't be easy, Jack.'

'I realise that.'

'Whenever you go into Hotten, I'll be wondering if you're calling to see her. Whenever you say you're going to see about replacing a tractor or buying some new heifers or calling on the bank manager, I'll be wondering if you are lying to me. If you come back smelling of curry or cigarette smoke, I'll be wondering if you've been out with her, having a meal or a drink in a pub.'

She paused to let him absorb her words, then continued, 'If you're late back home for any reason, or if you have to stay away overnight, then I'll be asking myself whether you are with her. That's the state you've left me in, Jack – and it's your fault, not mine.'

'I know, I've been a real bastard, and I want to make it up to you. But first, I do want you to trust me, Pat.'

'I know you do, and I want to trust you, Jack. I trusted you in the past, before this, but now, well, I'll need time, so don't try to rush me. I know you'll have to see Karen from time to time because of your work, but every time you do, I'll be on edge, worried, wondering if it will all flare up again . . .'

'No, it won't,' he said with some conviction.

But Pat was not so sure. 'I'll go and get on with that washing,' she said.

'And I'll get up to those sheep on the fells; some of that strong Pennine air will clear my brain, I reckon,' and he suddenly took her in his arms and kissed her. 'I do love you, Pat, I really do – and I always have.'

She said nothing as she turned away and began the walk back to the farm house. Jack watched her for a few moments, and then shouted, 'Pat?'

She halted and turned to face him.

'Yes?'

'How about a weekend away? Just you and me. To start all over again?'

She nodded vigorously. 'I'd like that,' she smiled.

For Amos Brearly, landlord and proprietor of the Woolpack Inn, Beckindale, Christmas had been a time of turmoil in what he normally regarded as an ocean of reasonable calm. The chief problem had been the absence of his partner, Henry Wilks, who had spent the holiday in Italy with his daughter Marian, her Italian husband Paolo, and his grandson Niccolò. Before leaving, Henry had helped Amos make the pre-Christmas arrangements, but Amos had had to recruit temporary bar staff in order to cope with the rush of orders. Charlie Grimthorpe had been recommended by the brewery, but in Amos's opinion, he lacked the style and professionalism required for an inn of the Woolpack's quality and reknown. The customers had felt the same.

Then Doreen from the Malt Shovel caused him problems; that was all Seth Armstrong's doing. When Seth had discovered Amos was to alone over the festive season, he let it be known to the voluptuous barmaid from Ernie Shuttleworth's establishment that Amos needed help. Doreen was officially on holiday, but had needed some extra cash for her Christmas spending, and with Seth's encouragement (reinforced by a campaign organised by Seth and some of the Woolpack's less discerning customers), she had offered her temporary services to Amos. Any doubts on his part had been dispelled by the swell of bar opinion, and a vote, again organised by Seth, had left Amos with no option other than to employ Doreen.

To avoid making Ernie suspicious, she had then moved into the Woolpack, taking over Henry's bedroom, and filling the bedroom with her underwear, lotions and strong-scented soaps. She had left only mintues before Henry's return and Amos knew Mr Wilks suspected him of having had a woman in his rooms!

Mind, Amos said to himself, Doreen had certainly brought in the customers . . . he chuckled as he thought of all the Malt Shovel's customers crowding into the Woolpack's bar over the festive season. Takings had been excellent, even if the woman had caused Amos to blush from time to time, to say nothing of having to endure some coarse jokes from the less sophisticated of the customers she had attracted. But Henry was now back in harness and things were back to normal.

However, there was one matter of momentous importance which had soon to be settled, and in Amos's mind it was a way of getting his own back on Seth for the Doreen business. It was the forthcoming election for the presidency of the Beckindale Allotments and Horticultural Society. He knew that Seth, as the current president, was expecting an uncontested election. But Amos planned to halt Seth in his tracks by ensuring that he, Mr Amos Brearly, beat him at the polls. The contest would be solely between him and Seth, and Amos knew that he and he alone could boast the superior qualities that were required for such a demanding and prestigious post. Nevertheless, some careful electioneering would be necessary.

Amos decided that a good presidential candidate should be seen to care for the environment, have an encyclopaedic knowledge of allotment cultivation, and an endless capacity for excellent, sustained work in difficult circumstances, such as weeding one's allotment in all weathers. It was to prove himself in all these areas that Amos became a beekeeper, or, as he preferred to refer to himself, an apiarist. Honey from bees was, after all, one of the most natural ways of food production, he would be seen by the other allotment users as a specialist in the subject, and looking after bees involved endless dedication and sensitivity. How could they fail to elect him president?

He joined Hotten Beekeepers' Association, bought himself some protective clothing, a smoke gun and a book about making honey, then set about obtaining a hive of bees. The Amos Brearly apiary was established on the allotments in due course and Amos began to discuss his latest passion in glowing terms.

It was Seth who first noticed the hive on the allotments and rushed to the Woolpack to discuss the matter.

'First things first, Amos, a pint please. Now,

second thing – what's that on your allotment? A temple of the gods or a safe for your carrots?'

'You could say it was a temple to the *food* of the gods, Seth Armstrong. It's my way of helping conservation, ensuring that our plants continue through fertilisation, if that's not too strong a word for this establishment, and at the same time I shall be rewarded with nectar of the gods, Seth. Honey. I am about to become a beekeeper, an apiarist, tha knows.'

'Apiarist, Amos?

'Aye, now us with a literary turn of mind can appreciate and understand such terms, Seth. Not that I'd expect you to know such refined things. Keeping an apiary is an art, tha knows, only being understood by those with higher intelligence, Seth Armstrong, so that rules you out.'

'So you're keeping bees on your allotment?' asked Seth.

'I am; they will enhance my allotment and they will fertilise the flora of the district. It's the sort of stylish move one would expect from a future president, Seth Armstrong.'

'And they'll break our allotment rules, Amos, and that's summat no prospective president should do.'

'Break the allotment rules, Seth? Whatever are you talking about?'

'Livestock, Amos. Rule 26(b). No allotment holder may keep, tend or accommodate any form of livestock on his/her allotment.'

Amos beamed. 'Then check on t'interpretation section, Seth. Last page, under "definitions". It says, "The term livestock shall not include honey bees

92

kept in a hive constructed and maintained in accordance with the recommendations of the British Beekeepers' Assoiacation." And I'll have you know that my apiary is in conformity with the rules of the B.B.A.'

'You're not serious, are you, Amos, about being a future president? I mean, I've been president for years . . .'

'Aye, well, some of us thought it was time for a change at the top, Seth, and I reckoned it was time to appoint somebody of stature, somebody with breeding, who'll keep his allotment tidy and well cultivated . . .'

Seth reflected upon his own weed-enveloped patch. 'Aye, well, I have been busy, Amos.'

'And so have I, Seth Armstrong – and doing double my work during the absence of my partner.'

'Aye, and getting up to all manner o' tricks with that Doreen, eh? Sleeping at the Woolpack each night; we know all about it, Amos. There's folks hereabouts who reckon she did you a power o' good, put a sparkle in your eyes, they said, even if it's not the sort o' conduct I'd expect of a future president . . .'

'Now, I'll have no such slander in this establishment, Seth Armstrong. Doreen were here to work and that's what she did. And she got paid for what she did.'

'So they say, Amos, so they say,' chuckled Seth, but Amos missed the barb in Seth's remarks. Seth continued, 'So you're putting up for president, eh. Well, I think that needs a challenge, Amos. As of

93

now, I'm going to campaign for the post and I hereby give you notice of my intentions!'

'And I reciprocate!' beamed Amos.

Seth's moustache bristled as he contemplated the challenge presented by Amos, then he said, 'I'll have a head start, anyroad, Amos.'

'Really?' Amos put his nose into the air in a pretence of being uninterested.

'Aye, I'm organising the NY Estates staff spring annual outing and we're going to Cleethorpes. I've a bus laid on and everybody on that bus'll vote for me, because I'll make sure they have t'best outing of their lives, Turner included.'

'Mr Turner is not a member of our Allotment Association, Seth, so he can't vote.'

'But he can exert influence, Amos, like Mr Hinton and folks of standing like that.'

'When it comes to folks of standing, Seth Armstrong, there's nobody can rival a Brearly. Personality. That's what catches votes. President Brearly, B.A.H.S. I can see it now.'

'President Armstrong, L.P.B.H.C.A.D.R.H.A.A.S, more like,' grinned Seth.

'And what might all that jumble mean?' asked Amos.

'Life President Beckindale, Hotten, Connelton And District Royal Horticultural And Allotment Society,' beamed Seth. 'Cos in my next presidential year, I intend to expand our interests and gain royal approval and patronage.'

'If you become the next president!'

'*When* I become the next president, Amos,' and Seth walked out to begin his campaign. He was

94

already mentally compiling a list of likely voters whom he could persuade with regular gifts of game from the estate.

And Amos was dreaming of a presidential campaign aided by jars of purest Brearly honey made by happy bees from the flora of Beckindale and district, and processed in the Amos Brearly apiary, the finest for miles around.

As the presidential campaign got underway, Alan Turner walked into his office at Home Farm one day and it was evident that he was in a foul mood. Mrs Bates tried to ignore this as she dealt with the morning mail.

'When you left last night, you asked me to remind you about today's main job, Mr Turner. The analysis of the quarterly accounts. For Head Office. It's the deadline tomorrow, she said.'

'Yes, yes, Mrs Bates. You make a start, and then I'll check them with you. I'll, er, glance through them.'

'They are important, Mr Turner, they need some examination by you, detailed examination, that is, and comment.'

'And so does this, Mrs Bates.' He was waving a letter in the air. 'You know what this is?'

'Er, no,' she had to say.

'This, Mrs Bates, is the sum total of more than twenty-three years of marriage for me. Quite an impressive legacy, eh?'

'Surely things have been shared out equally, Mr Turner?'

'Equally in favour of that ex-wife of mine, you

mean, with the scheming of her solicitor and accountants. Just because she runs a business and I've been on a salary, it means she has got the lot, Mrs Bates. Well, almost the lot, because of her high income. High now, that is. I kept her when she started, but no one seems to take note of that. She's won the house, most of the furniture and a whopping sum to be paid by me into her bank account every month. It's not at all fair, Mrs Bates. Divorce is heavily biased against the husband, all in favour of the wife. I mean, I did support her during our early years, and I am paying Amanda's school fees, I paid Terence's as well, and now I'm helping him at university. Grants don't go far, you know . . .'

'But, Mr Turner, you must have got something.'

'Mrs Bates, I am very angry about this and I have no intention of starting a discussion about the merits or otherwise of our crazy divorce laws.'

'As you say, Mr Turner. Now, these figures.'

'Er, yes, now did I mention that speech I am to make this evening? To the Hotten Young Farmers Club? It's their annual dinner and I am the guest speaker – at least I'll get a nice meal out of them. Anyway, I have drafted a speech, so perhaps you would type it out for me? Double-spacing for clarity, paragraph headings in bold, usual thing.'

'But the figures, Mr Turner . . .'

'Yes, yes. You do those while I'm amending my speech, and then I will check the figures while you are re-typing the speech after my amendments. It's all very simple, Mrs Bates, a matter of organising one's tasks to fit the time available.'

'Yes, Mr Turner.'

For Caroline Bates, the day was something of a trial, with Turner constantly returning to the subject of his divorce, sometimes ringing up friends, acquaintances and financial experts for their advice, and at the same time dismissing Caroline's efforts to make him concentrate upon his work. There was no doubt the outcome of his divorce had upset him and she had never seen him so bitter. She only hoped this did not detract from the speech he was to make this evening.

Somehow, the required analysis was finished on time and he did make his own assessment of the figures; he did complete his speech too, and she had to agree that it was a well-drafted text which raised many salient points about the future of farming in Britain. But when he left to drive to Hotten that evening, he was still in a very bad mood. She hoped that the dinner tonight and the companionship of the Young Farmers Club would cheer him up.

Jackie Merrick had decided to have a night out without Alison. He had heard of a dance in a barn between Connelton and Hotten, a large place where there was to be a live group with dancing, drinks and plenty of food.

'There'll be those nurses from Hotten General,' he said to Mike West. 'They get bus trips out to village dances, to meet new blokes, so I reckon we should go and see what they're like.'

'Is your Sandie going? I fancy her, Jackie. Any chance of persuading her to go?'

'If she goes, you don't. I've only got the motor

97

bike. But I wanted a lads' outing, Mike. Just you and me.'

'What about Archie, then?' asked Mike.

'Yeh, well, tell him an' all, he might make his own way there. Is his van still on the road?'

'If it is, I'm not riding in it!' laughed Mike. 'OK, Jackie old son. Barn dance it is. What time?'

'I'll see you in the Woolpack at eight, we'll go from there.'

And so it was that Jackie Merrick, with Mike West perched on the pillion of his old motor cycle, set off to visit this dance. When they arrived, it was packed with other young people.

'Great, eh? Hey, there's Archie, over there with those lasses. Come on, let's go.'

They enjoyed the evening tremendously, the lads had lots of sandwiches and cakes, Jackie having only a couple of drinks, not enough to make him incapable of driving home, and they met two nurses who joined in their fun.

When it was all over, and when they had kissed their new friends goodnight, Mike said, 'Are you fit to drive home, Jackie?'

'Course I am,' he responded. 'One pint of beer, and several non-alcoholic lagers! Hop aboard, Mike, the night air will sober you up!'

And so, at around quarter past midnight, they set off to return to Beckindale.

Jackie drove steadily, not wishing to court the attention of any patrolling police car nor to risk anything happening to his old machine; it had done well on this trip, although it could be temperamental if it rained. Damp sometimes caused the spark plug to misfire and he knew the wiring to both the headlight and rear light was not too sound. The lights had a tendency to cut out on bumpy roads and so he drove very steadily, carefully avoiding potholes and rough patches.

'You'll have to pull up!' shouted Mike after a while. 'I need to get behind a hedge!'

'You went before we set off, didn't you?' cried Jackie.

'Aye, but I'll have to go again, it's all that beer. It goes through me like nobody's business.'

'Can't you wait till we get back to Demdyke Cottage?' called Jackie. 'Sometimes if I stop this old bike, I have trouble starting it again when the engine's hot.'

'Then keep it running . . . look, Jackie, you'll have to stop. I'm bursting, honest . . .'

'There's a wood just along here,' Jackie finally agreed. 'I'll stop there and you dash into the trees.'

'Thanks, mate.'

Jackie eased to a halt at the roadside, his bike bumping along the rough grass verge. And all the lights went out.

'Now look what you've done!' Jackie cried. 'I knew this would happen . . .'

'We'll soon fix them, it'll be a loose wire.' Mike was already scrambling into the trees in the darkness. 'Hang on, won't be a tick . . .'

Jackie remained astride his motor bike as he fiddled first with the ignition key and then with the light switches, feeling along the length of the wires which ran beneath his petrol tank to the rear light. He shook the wires – and the lights came on.

'Hey, look at you!' he called, turning the front wheel to direct a spotlight upon his pal among the trees. But the lights went out again. And it was then that the sound of a Land Rover reached them. Mike was concluding the purpose of his halt when he saw the approaching vehicle; it was driving fast, perhaps a shade too fast for this country lane, and it was bearing down on Jackie.

'Jackie!' he shouted. 'Jackie, look out, behind you . . .'

Jackie turned.

He saw the twin headlights only yards behind him; he saw the startled white face of the man behind the wheel . . . and then, in what appeared to be desperately slow motion, he and his bike were hurled into the air, the bike landing in the ditch with a terrible rending of metal.

The air filled with the stench of flooding petrol as the Land Rover screeched to a halt.

But Jackie knew no more. He lay unconscious in the ditch with blood oozing from his shattered body.

Chapter Six

Alan Turner stormed from the Land Rover, fully intent on venting his anger and vengeance upon whatever irresponsible person had parked the unlit motor cycle in his path. He saw Mike, pale-faced and horrified, rushing from the trees, and then Jackie Merrick, still and bleeding in the ditch.

'Oh my God!' Turner breathed as he stooped to examine Jackie in the glow from the Land Rover's headlamps. With surprising dexterity, he crouched at the boy's side and ran his hands lightly over Jackie's body, placing his head close to Jackie's mouth to listen to his breathing. It sounded as if he was choking and so Turner opened Jackie's mouth and inserted his fingers to free his tongue from the back of his throat where it was restricting his breathing.

'I daren't move him, he's too badly injured,' he said quietly. 'He needs skilled treatment. Mike, be quick about it, go and ring for the ambulance and tell them a doctor is needed. Stress that we need a professional opinion here. Then call the police. This is urgent, Mike, really urgent. There's a cottage just back there, round the corner, you might have to knock them out of bed.'

Mike ran. He realised with relief that Alan Turner seemed to know precisely what he was doing.

Turner had seen that if Jackie were moved without

skilled attention the effect might be fatal. What if the boy had sustained spinal injuries or other internal damage? Normally in an accident of this kind he would have turned Jackie into a half-prone position, his head on one side on the ground to prevent him swallowing his tongue or inhaling vomit if he were sick, and choking. But recognising the awkward position in which Jackie was lying, the unnatural angle of his pelvis and legs, he knew that this was not a situation for amateur first-aid treatment. All he could do was to cover the boy with a travelling rug from the Land Rover and stay by his side, whispering words of comfort.

Some five minutes later, Mike returned, panting and anxious.

'You got them?' asked Turner.

'Yeh,' Mike said. 'I said a doctor was needed, t'ambulance is coming, they said they'd ring the police, it's automatic for traffic accidents. Shouldn't we lift him out of that ditch, Mr Turner? Put him in your Land Rover where it's warm, or something?' He looked down upon his injured pal.

'No, Mike. He's too badly hurt; he needs skilled medical attention, just look at his legs, listen to his breathing . . .'

'You know what you're doing then?'

'I know a little first aid, Mike; one has to learn basic skills when one is in my position . . .'

'You were going a bit fast, weren't you? Coming like hell along that lane, Mr Turner.'

'The bike had no lights on, Mike – I had no chance . . .'

Mike did not reply. He recognised the truth in that, so he bent down to examine his friend, knowing that if he had not persuaded Jackie to stop, this accident would never have occurred.

'He looks bad, Mr Turner, isn't there summat we should be doing? We're just standing around while he's bleeding . . .'

'It's not arterial blood, Mike, it's not pumping his life away, and so long as he can continue breathing, there is nothing else we can do, nothing else we *dare* do. For God's sake don't try to move him . . .'

'Why are they so long?' Mike was now pacing up and down, looking at his watch as Jackie began to groan and tried to move. 'It doesn't take all this time to get from Hotten . . .'

'I must stop Jackie moving, he needs to lie absolutely still. They'll be here just as soon as they can, Mike, and Jackie will get the very best treatment.' But in his heart, Turner was a very worried man. He could see that Jackie was seriously injured, and yet he was helpless to do anything further for him. All that could be done here, had been done.

In the glow from the Land Rover's lights, he knelt at Jackie's side with Mike looking over his shoulder, making sure Jackie was as comfortable as possible, wiping a little blood from the boy's mouth and reassuring Mike that his pal would survive. Jackie's crash helmet had been thrown off by the impact; he'd loosened the strap while examining his lights, but there was no blood from Jackie's ears, an indication that the base of his skull was probably not fractured, and the rest of his head did not appear to have been damaged. Jackie's moaning increased and, for a moment, he opened his eyes to stare wildly about, blinking at the harsh light.

'You're going to be fine, Jackie,' Turner soothed him. Jackie only groaned again and tried to turn his head, but Turner said, 'Don't try to move, Jackie. Just lie still, help is on the way . . .'

'Where the hell is that ambulance?' Mike was pacing up and down the road, returning to his friend every few seconds, peering up the lane into the darkness, feeling utterly helpless as Jackie lay suffering. Then, with immense relief, he saw the flashing blue lights approaching, in the distance, behind the trees.

'They're coming,' Mike said. Thank God . . . how is he?'

'Semi-conscious,' said Turner. 'But he's tough, Mike, and he'll survive.'

But even Alan Turner was not sure that this would be the case. He waited with patience but deep anxiety as the blue lights grew closer. As they turned the corner into the stretch of road that led to the stationary Land Rover, he saw that a police car was leading the ambulance to the scene. Within minutes, the entire location was alive with uniformed men. They worked efficiently and without any fuss. The still night air of the quiet country lane filled with the crackle of voices from the radios of both the police car and the ambulance. The scene was bathed in the curious blue of the flashing lights, and the police car shone its headlights onto the verge near where Jackie lay as the ambulance men organised their equipment – a firm stretcher, which had to be placed beneath Jackie with the minimum of lifting, a pneumatic splint to cushion his battered body against any movement.

A doctor was with them; he was on emergency call-out from the Hotten group practice, and had followed the ambulance and police car to the scene. Before Jackie was moved, the doctor made a careful examination and then addressed Turner and Mike.

'You've not moved him?' he asked, with concern in his voice.

'No, I thought it best not to!' Turner answered. 'Except his head, I turned that to free his tongue . . .'

'Excellent, well, I think your actions will have saved this lad's life,' and then the doctor turned to Mike. 'You were on the pillion, I take it?'

'Yes, but I'd gone into the woods for a jimmy-riddle,' said Mike.

'So you've no injuries, nor you, sir?' he addressed Turner.

'Er, no. The motor bike was stationary, you see. I was in that Land Rover, quite safe, not even a knock on the head.'

'Right.' The doctor addressed the ambulance crew. 'Into the ambulance with him, carefully, he's very badly hurt, a fractured pelvis, I think, or perhaps the femur, and some internal injuries, intestines maybe, with a possibility of some haemorrhaging. You'll need that pneumatic splint and I don't want him altered from his present position when you do the lift. Take him to casualty and drive carefully. I'll follow you.' And so the ambulancemen got to work with their stretcher and blankets as Sergeant MacArthur approached Alan Turner.

'All in good hands now, Mr Turner. So what happened? I'll have to compile an accident report, you understand, so I'll need some details from you.'

'Yes, yes, of course, Sergeant.'

'Can we talk now or shall I see you at your office? You will be in a state of shock you know, once this is over. I suggest you go home and have a hot, sweet drink.'

'I can feel the shock coming on now, Sergeant. Perhaps I'd better get home.'

'Your vehicle is fit to drive, is it?' Sergeant MacArthur was prowling around it, examining it for signs of damage in the light of his own torch.

'Yes, surprisingly little damage, superficial marks, that's all.'

'I'll have to ask you for a breath test before you leave, Mr Turner. Standard procedure in cases like this, you understand. Now, have you been drinking this evening?'

'Yes, but not to excess, I can assure you. I had a glass of wine at dinner with the Hotten Young Farmers Club and a sherry before the meal. That's all.'

The sergeant assembled the breathalyser kit and asked Turner to blow into the tube; he did so and when MacArthur examined it, he said, 'Aye, Mr Turner, you have been drinking, it shows up green, but you're not over the limit, you'll be glad to know.'

'Yes, well, I am a responsible person, you know.'

'And you, Mike,' the sergeant now addressed him. 'Were you driving that bike?'

'No, Jackie was. I was on the pillion.'

'And you'd stopped here?'

'Yes, I went for a pee in the woods and Jackie was sat astride the bike, waiting for me. He was on the proper side of the road . . .'

'Without lights,' added Turner. 'There were no lights on that bike, well, no back lights, otherwise I'd have seen it and avoided it.'

'Is that true?' MacArthur asked Mike.

'He was having trouble with the lights, they went out when he pulled up; they were going on and off and he was trying to fix 'em when I was in the wood.'

'Fair enough,' said Sergeant MacArthur. 'I'll see you tomorrow as well, Mike, for a formal statement. Had Jackie been drinking?'

'Alcohol-free lagers, he was very responsible,' Mike said.

'We can't breath-test him in the state he's in – anyway, our traffic department will come and collect his bike and we'll test the wiring. Mind, in the state it's in now, it might not be easy to find out a great deal. And our lads'll have to test your Land Rover, Mr Turner – brakes, steering and so on. Tomorrow morning at Home Farm?'

As the sergeant finished his preliminary enquiries, the ambulancemen tenderly loaded Jackie into their vehicle and, having obtained Jackie's full name and address from Mike, set off for Hotten General Hospital. The sergeant measured the scene of the accident, pinpointing the position of each vehicle, and then said, 'You'll take Mike home, will you, Mr Turner? It'd be a help.'

107

'Yes, of course. Er, Sergeant, someone will have to inform Jack and Pat Sugden . . .'

'I'll see to that, Mr Turner. I'll do it straight away – Jackie was living at Demdyke, wasn't he, Mike?'

'Yes, so they won't know he's late home.'

The formalities of the accident completed, Alan Turner, with Mike West sitting stunned at his side, drove home to Beckindale.

'Er, Mike,' said Turner as they motored along. 'Thanks for being honest with the sergeant – about the lights, I mean.'

'It's the least I can do, Mr Turner – it was the truth. Anyway, you saved Jackie's life, didn't you? Knowing not to move him and keep his breathing clear.'

'One finds oneself responding in an emergency,' he said quietly. 'Now, I'll drop you off and then get home. I'm coming over all shaky now.'

'Me too, Mr Turner. You know, if I hadn't made Jackie stop . . .'

'Don't blame yourself, Mike; it was an accident, and no one's to blame.'

But Mike would always blame himself for this. And suppose Jackie never recovered?

The knocking persisted. Eventually, it penetrated the slumbering mind of Pat Sugden who was snuggled down in bed with Jack, her legs and arms entwined with his.

She frowned in the darkness, trying to see the time on the bedside clock, but the hammering continued.

108

'Jack.' She dug him with her elbow. 'Jack, there's somebody at the door.'

'Huh?'

'Jack.' She was wide-awake now. 'Jack, somebody's knocking . . .'

Jack struggled to gather his wits, as he fought his way out of a deep sleep, and then listened as the loud banging continued. Then, wrapping himself in his dressing gown, he struggled into his slippers and, shivering against the chill of the night, put on the light and went downstairs. The knocking continued as he switched on the kitchen light.

'All right, I'm coming,' he shouted at the anonymous caller. 'Hang on a minute.'

As he opened the door, a cold blast of night air swept in, causing him to fold his dressing gown tightly around himself as he faced Sergeant MacArthur.

'Jack,' said the sergeant. 'Sorry to knock you up.'

'Important, is it?'

'Aye,' said the sergeant, stepping inside as Jack motioned him indoors with a wave of his hand. As he entered, Pat came downstairs clutching her dressing gown about her slender body. Her face bore signs of concern as she saw the big policeman in the kitchen.

'Pat,' said MacArthur. 'Look, I'm sorry to get you out of bed, both of you, but it's your Jackie . . .'

'Jackie?' cried Pat.

'Aye.' MacArthur was accustomed to breaking bad news. 'Sit down, both of you.'

They obeyed without further question as he settled on a kitchen chair beside the table.

'Jackie's had an accident,' he said. 'He's been knocked down and he's in hospital in Hotten, alive and in good hands.'

'Knocked down?' Jack puzzled over the choice of words. 'Knocked off his bike, you mean? Has he run into something?'

'He'd parked up while his mate went into the wood near Carr Bottoms – he was sitting astride when another vehicle ran into the bike and knocked Jackie off. He's in hospital, as I said, in casualty.'

'He's not . . . well . . . likely to die, or anything, is he?' Pat asked.

'He's in a very bad way, I've got to say that.' MacArthur was honest. 'But he's tough and he was well looked after at the time.'

'Can we go and see him?' was her next question.

'He's in intensive care, Pat. I'd ring the hospital before going over there. You'll not see him if you go now.'

'Who knocked him off?' was Jack's next question, sensing that the sergeant seemed reluctant to pass on that information at this stage.

'Alan Turner . . .'

'Drunk, was he?' cried Jack. 'My God, if that man has done any permanent harm to Jackie, I'll strangle him with my bare hands, so I will . . .'

'Jack, before you do something you'll regret, you'll find Turner's prompt action saved Jackie's life. Even the doctor said that.'

'But how could he run down a lad on a parked bike, for God's sake?'

'There's the question of whether Jackie's lights were working, Jack. I've got my report to complete so I'm not entirely sure myself yet. Anyway, look, Jackie's in very good hands, he's alive and he's fit and strong. He *is* in a fairly bad way, I'd be lying if I tried to tell you any different, so you'd best ring the hospital to get the latest on him,' and Sergeant MacArthur prepared to leave.

'Thanks for coming to tell us,' Pat said.

'I'm just glad it wasn't worse news,' said MacArthur. 'Oh, and before the rumours get flying around, Turner wasn't drunk. I breath-tested him, and he wasn't over the limit, or anywhere near it.'

Jack did not respond to this piece of news but nodded his thanks and said, 'I'll ring the hospital straight away.'

In spite of the hour, Jack and Pat woke the others and went to the hospital, and after explaining Jackie's relationship to them, a query being raised by his Merrick surname, Jack asked to see the consultant surgeon as he sought the truth of their son's condition.

'The resuscitation machine is precautionary, Mr Sugden,' he explained. 'Jackie's breathing is causing some concern, although he is by no means at a danger level. His broken ribs will be making it painful to take deep breaths and he is in a state of deep shock, so we are giving him a little assistance, that's all. His head is not injured, other than some superficial bruising, although he does have severe concussion. There is no damage to his brain, we can be sure of that.'

'That's a relief!'

'The biggest problem is the damage to his pelvis.

Mr Sugden, and to his left leg. I'm going to be honest with you by saying it will be a long time before he walks again . . .'

Pat covered her face with her hands while Jack sat, impassive and angry.

'What's that mean?' asked Pat.

'It means that we will keep him in hospital for several months, Mrs Sugden, and that major surgery is required. We will begin the emergency operations within the next two or three hours, and Jackie will be on his back in this hospital for many weeks or even months afterwards.'

'But he will get better?' Jack was seeking reassurance now.

'He will, but it will take a long, long time,' said the surgeon. Pat began to cry as Jack put his arm around her.

'Come on, luv, we'll come back and see him soon. You know our Jackie, he'll make it.'

It was six o'clock in the morning when they returned to Emmerdale to find Annie and Sandie waiting anxiously at the farm, with Matt and Dolly at the kitchen table. They were sitting with empty tea cups and Matt was about to go out to begin the milking.

Jack informed them of Jackie's present condition and also explained a little of the circumstances of the accident as he knew them.

'So there's nowt we can do?' asked Matt.

'Not just now,' said Jack. 'We've not even seen him ourselves yet, he's in intensive care.'

'We're going to be short-handed on the farm, Jack,' Matt said. 'We could get by if it was only to

112

be a day or two, but, well, it'll be months before Jackie's right again.'

Jack sighed heavily as Matt made out his case.

'I mean, there's lambing for one thing and there's his turns in the milking schedules . . .'

'We'll have a meeting about that, Matt. It might mean taking on a paid labourer, eh? Give it some thought over the next day or two, then we'll get it sorted out.'

'There's bound to be somebody wanting work,' said Annie. And so the routine of Emmerdale Farm continued, with Jackie's appalling injuries casting unhappiness over the family.

There was more gloom in the office of NY Estates at Home Farm. When Mrs Bates arrived for work that morning, she found her boss slumped in his chair, unshaven, and with his clothes all crumpled and awry. There was an empty whisky bottle on his desk, and an upturned glass near his right hand.

'Mr Turner!' she cried. 'Are you all right?'

He shook his head in his misery, unable or unwilling to respond to her question. She was sure he was not ill, but suffering from a monumental hangover, so she went across to her own desk and sat down to begin work. She remained anxious about him as she uncovered her word processor and assembled the post for opening but all the time she was glancing across at Turner.

'Would a coffee help, Mr Turner?'

'Oh, er, yes. Yes, that is a good idea, Mrs Bates. Yes, very strong and hot. Black, I think . . .' He staggered over to fetch it.

She was even more convinced he'd had a hectic night at the Hotten Young Farmers Club dinner and that this was a legacy of a heavy drinking session. Who'd brought him home, she wondered? The Land Rover was parked outside. She decided to mention the work outstanding he'd promised to help her with.

'If you're up to it, Mr Turner, there are those stock returns that Head Office wants. I have done a preliminary set for you to look at, with a few queries I've found myself . . .'

'Mrs Bates.' He returned to his desk bearing a cup of coffee and sank into his chair. 'I'm sorry if I am not very communicative this morning . . . I've been here all night, at my desk, alone with my thoughts . . . terrible thoughts, Mrs Bates.'

'Why? Mr Turner, what's matter?'

'I think I might have killed somebody, Mrs Bates. I really do . . .'

'Good God, when?'

And he told her his story, highlighting the fact that Jackie's bike was not showing any lights and explaining how impossible it had been to avoid a collision. She listened with deep concern. When he'd finished, she asked, 'Have you telephoned the hospital to see how Jackie's progressing?'

'I did ring before you came in, Mrs Bates, but they were guarded about what they said. "Mr Merrick is in intensive care and is very poorly" – that's all they would say, and I know what "very poorly" means. I did press them for more, using my authority, I might add, to gain access to the ward sister, and she said he was on a resuscitation machine.

114

Breathing difficulties, apparently. It means he could die and if that happens, then I could be held responsible . . .'

She listened in horror as he described the accident all over again, and found herself in sympathy with him.

'I'll ring Emmerdale,' she said. 'To ask after Jackie, to see if there's anything we can do.'

'I should think Jack Sugden wants to shoot me on sight now . . . I mean, it's not as if it was my fault, Mrs Bates. I know that lad and me have had our differences, but this is awful, I mean I'm no ogre, . . .'

Mrs Bates did ring Emmerdale Farm and found herself speaking to Pat. She asked after Jackie and learned that he was in intensive care, but that he was in no danger. His breathing had now been regulated and he was as comfortable as possible, although he would be having an operation on his pelvis some time during the day. Caroline Bates thanked Pat and wished Jackie a speedy recovery. Turner was very relieved to hear this.

'I'd do anything to see that lad fit again, Mrs Bates,' he said. 'I know what the Sugdens must be going through. I have a son of my own, you know, and I can imagine what's going through Jack and Pat's mind.'

'Shall we settle down to those returns, Mr Turner?' she said. 'You need something to take your mind off last night.'

'Yes, yes of course. So what's first?'

'Head Office is querying the expenditure on those

Swaledale ewes, Mr Turner.' He groaned at their pettiness.

News of Jackie's accident swept through Beckindale that day and there were the inevitable rumours that Turner had been drunk at the time. Many of the villagers sent fruit and get-well cards for Jackie, gestures that Pat found very moving. She and Jack would visit the hospital that evening, although it was by no means certain that Jackie would be fit enough to receive them or even be aware of their presence.

Seth was most distressed at the news of his young friend and so was Archie Brooks, while Mr Hinton felt it might be an idea to hold prayers for Jackie during the forthcoming Sunday services. Amos and Wilks found themselves discussing the matter, with Amos pontificating about the dangers of motor bikes, while Henry wondered how the family would cope at the farm without Jackie's capable help.

'I'd best pop up and have a word with them,' he announced.

When he arrived, he found Mike West already there. He was having a cup of coffee with Sandie who had been given the morning off work to visit the hospital and support her mother. Mike was telling her all about the accident, how he felt he was to blame and how well Mr Turner had coped. Sandie listened to him and felt sorry for this young man who, it seemed, had just learnt a very tough lesson about life. He asked if Sandie would go out with him, just for a drink, to cheer him up. Not wishing to begin a romance, but anxious to assure Mike that no one held him to blame, Sandie agreed.

Wilks talked with Annie and Pat in the parlour, and after receiving their report on Jackie's condition and the length of time it would take before Jackie was able to work again, Henry offered any help he could give. Pat thanked him.

'The main problem,' she said, 'will be the evening milking when we're visiting Jackie and Matt's busy with his lambing. Me and Jack will take turns, obviously, and Dolly's always a marvellous help when we're short.'

'So you'd like me to step in and do a spot of milking?' he offered with a sparkle in his eye. 'And mebbe a bit of swilling out, ploughing or whatever . . . you know, I could even get to like that! A life in the open air – that's just what I need, and it'll be a change from hearing Amos's yarns at the bar of the Woolpack!'

'And how will Amos cope?' asked Annie.

'Well, he coped when I was in Rome,' Henry chuckled. 'He got a woman in then! Happen he'll cope now in the quiet season – besides, I'll be around to help with the cellar work and so on.'

'So I can tell Jack the good news?' smiled Pat.

'You can,' agreed Henry. 'So when do I start?'

'Tonight?' laughed Pat. 'At milking time?'

'I'd best find some suitable clothes,' he grinned. 'Then mebbe Jack'll show me how to work that milking machine.'

Henry and Mike left at the same time, with Henry offering to give the lad a lift into the village. The women watched them leave, Annie pleased that Henry had offered his services while Sandie was thinking over Mike's request for comfort.

And then the telephone rang. Annie answered it.

'Sandie, it's for you,' she said. 'It's the prison.'

'Prison?' she puzzled, picking up the handset. 'Hello, this is Sandie Merrick,' she announced.

A woman's voice at the other end said, 'Oh, this is the Governor's secretary, Miss Merrick. You are Tom Merrick's next-of-kin, I understand?'

'Yes, I'm his daughter,' she replied.

'Well, Mr Merrick is being released next Tuesday at 10am,' said the voice. Perhaps you would like to come and meet him?'

Chapter Seven

Sandie drove alone to the prison to collect her father. When he emerged from the giant doors, he looked pale and thin after his months of incarceration, although he insisted he was fitter than he'd been for a long time, what with abstinence from alcohol, and regular work-outs in the prison gym.

Father and daughter embraced and she took his meagre belongings and placed them in the boot of her car. She said she'd drive him to Emmerdale because Annie had offered to give him his dinner today, and had even offered to accommodate him in either Grandad's room or at Demdyke until he sorted out his immediate future. As they drove away, Sandie told him of Jackie's accident.

The moment Tom Merrick learned of Jackie's injuries, he said he wanted to visit him. Sandie tried to explain that Jackie was in intensive care and that visitors were being discouraged at the moment; besides, any permitted visiting was for members of the immediate family only. But this made no impact upon her father.

'I brought that lad up, Sandie,' he said. 'So he's just as much mine as those Sugdens' – and he carries my name, remember. I'll drop you at the Mart, then I'll borrow your car, can I?'

'You'll be wasting your time, Dad,' she said. 'They've been very insistent about not tiring Jackie or upsetting him by too many visitors. Jack and Mum have hardly seen him.'

Tom thought for a moment, but it was clear that he was determined. 'If you don't try pushing your luck in this world, lass, you get nowhere,' he told her. 'And after doing extra time in that God-forsaken dump, I'm ready to see my family – even if some of 'em didn't come to see me as oft as they could.'

'If you hadn't had that fight with that chap in prison, you wouldn't have had to do extra time.' She implied it was his own fault. 'Besides, we did come, Dad, me and Jackie, Mum sometimes as well; we didn't ignore you and you know it.'

'Aye, well, it seemed a long, lonely time in there, Sandie, just for taking a few fish . . .'

'It was for all your other offences, Dad,' she said. 'You haven't exactly been an angel, have you?'

'I know, I know, I've been a bloody fool, Sandie, but I've paid for my mistakes. I'm going to behave from now on, you'll see, and I'm not getting involved with any more of Derek Warner's daft schemes. So can I borrow your car?'

'Of course you can.'

Having dropped Sandie off at Hotten Mart, Tom drove out to the hospital and parked, only to be told by a smart gentleman in a large Jaguar that, 'You can't park there, it's for consultants.'

'I'm going to consult with somebody,' was Tom's smiling response as he left the car and walked towards the wards. Inside, he found Jack and Pat also waiting.

'Tom!' Pat cried. 'What a surprise . . .'

She hurried to her former husband and hugged him, so pleased that he had made this visit his first priority upon release,

'Tom,' Jack smiled and shook Tom's hand. 'Glad to see you've got out of there.'

'How's Jackie?' Tom asked anxiously, brushing aside further formalities.

'He's still on the resuscitation machine,' Jack told him. 'The consultant's coming in this morning to examine him.'

'Can we see him?' asked Tom.

'Not yet, maybe later in the morning. We've got to wait until the consultant's finished his examination. That's why we're here.'

As they waited at the hospital, Tom was restless and aggravating, constantly upsetting the routine of the hospital by pressing the nurses for information, asking for cups of coffee, wanting to use the telephone to ring the oil rig at Aberdeen about a job, and in-between times telling Jack and Pat, and lots of other waiting visitors, about his treatment in prison. Jack smiled ruefully at his antics, but said nothing; Pat, however, was clearly overjoyed at having Tom for companionship at this moment, and she knew Jack would feel just a hint of jealousy, of competing for Jackie's smiles, perhaps . . .

An hour and a quarter passed before the consultant emerged to speak with them; when he came into the waiting room, Tom saw it was the man who had ticked him off for parking.

'My name is Mr Smale, Anthony Smale,' he said. 'I'm consultant surgeon, and I have been examining

Jackie . . . Jackie Merrick. Now, er, are you, er, all family?'

Without explaining to Smale the somewhat complicated relationships involved, Jack smiled and simply said, 'Yes, all of us.'

Smale sat on a chair beside Pat.

'Your son is a very strong and healthy young man,' he began. 'And that means he had a very good chance of recovery.'

'How is he?' interrupted Tom.

Smale looked at him, recognising him as the man who'd parked in the consultants' area, and smiled.

'If I said he was very well, I'd be lying.' He was honest, 'For a man with his injuries, he is rallying very well and we are all confident of his recovery. Now, he is still in intensive care; there has been some further complication with his breathing – some degree of lung embolism – and we need to clarify the position regarding that before we operate. An operation is still needed to repair his pelvic bones but there are other matters to settle first. We have already carried out some internal operations to stem bleeding. They have been successful.'

'He won't be a cripple, will he?' asked Jack.

'No, we feel not. It will be some months before he will walk again, and it is very fortunate he was not moved after the accident – the man who tended him did a superb job. What we have to do, is to use chromium pins to fasten his pelvic bones in a secure position so that nature can carry out the repairs. That takes a long time, and it cannot be rushed.'

Smale allowed these words to sink in before continuing. 'But in these cases – and there are many

of this kind involving young men and motor bikes –
we find there is a very good record of recovery. Full
mobility is achieved in most cases and there is every
reason to think Jackie will achieve this – but I stress
that it will take several months.

Now, I don't think we will have any trouble with
the bruises and cuts, and we hope to carry out the
operation on his pelvis soon, subject of course to a
satisfactory breathing capability. His left leg will
then be in plaster and he will be immobilised from
the waist down for several weeks.

After the operation, he will have to remain in bed
without moving that part of his body, and then he'll
use a wheelchair and after all that – I'm speaking of
months now – he will have to learn to walk all over
again. It is not going to be easy, for him or for you.
You will need extreme patience.'

No one spoke after these words, each sitting with
their own thoughts until Jack said, 'Then his injuries
really are serious? Very serious, I mean?'

'Yes,' said Mr Smale. 'Very serious. He is lucky
to be alive. Very lucky.'

Pat held her hand to her mouth to stop herself
from crying as she considered anew the enormity of
Jackie's injuries, and it was Tom who put his arm
around her shoulders. 'He's alive and he's strong,'
he said to her softly. 'He'll be back on his feet soon,
laughing and fit, you'll see.'

Pat sniffed back her tears and asked Smale, 'Can
we see him now?'

'He is conscious just at the moment, but under
immense stress. I can allow one minute – no more –

123

and just two of you, please. I cannot allow him to become excited or tired.'

Tom looked at Jack. For a long moment, Jack appeared to be pondering over who should make this visit, and them said, 'You go, Tom. With Pat.'

There were tears of gratitude in Tom's eyes as he and Pat followed the surgeon into the depths of the hospital.

Over coffee that same morning, Matt and Dolly were discussing the future of their own little family.

'I've been thinking, Matt,' Dolly said as they enjoyed these few moments alone. 'Mebbe it's time we tried for another bairn, a little brother or sister for Sam.'

'Aye, that accident does make you think. I mean, if Jackie had died . . .'

'That's what I mean,' she went on. 'You never know what the future holds. If owt happened to young Sam, we'd have nobody.'

'We've tried before, luv,' Matt sighed. 'Nowt happens. I mean, it's not as if we've been trying to avoid having more, but it just doesn't happen. You never get pregnant.'

'I thought I'd go and see a specialist,' said Dolly. 'Just to be sure there's nowt wrong with me.'

'Does that mean I'll have to go, an' all?' asked Matt.

'That'll depend on what happens with me,' she smiled. 'Look, do you agree? I mean, it is all right if I make an appointment, just for a check?'

'Aye, course it is.' He rose from his chair and

kissed her. 'You know, it would be nice having another, eh? It'd be somebody for little Sam to play with.'

'You really mean that?' She was delighted at his response. 'I thought you mightn't want another.'

'If you'd asked me last month, I might not have been so keen, but, well, seeing what can happen to a family makes you think, doesn't it?'

'It'd be so terrible if we lost Sam, wouldn't it?' She stood up and hugged Matt as he prepared to resume work. 'I mean, if we did finish up with nobody.'

'Then you fix an appointment,' he said.

This decision was just one outcome of Jackie's accident, which had had a profound effect upon many other people in Beckindale. Certainly it had become the talk of the Woolpack Inn, and it had thoroughly disturbed Archie Brooks, Jackie's left-wing revolutionary pal. He found difficulty in coping with the thought that a man as young as Jackie might be physically handicapped for life. But the incident had had the most impact on Mike West.

'I'm going to settle down,' he told Archie on a long walk one afternoon. 'Find meself a nice wife and a good job and settle down to a proper life.'

'You surprise me, Mike,' Archie said. 'There'll be no social justice in this world until folk like us fight for our rights not to work and not to be slaves of the capitalist system . . .'

'You talk a load of rot, Archie, you and your anarchistic beliefs. Family life, that's the root of all contentment and happiness in this world, good family life. I mean, suppose Jackie had had nobody

. . . nobody to love him, nobody special, just doctors and nurses to fix his legs and bring him his meals . . .'

'You'll never find work around here, Mike,' Archie said. 'Too many landowners around here, you know, keeping the proletariat down, they are.'

'Then I'll move away to find work, I'll get on my bike, as they say, to find something worthwhile so as some woman will be proud of me and'll want to marry me . . .'

'I thought you were a bit keen on Sandie Merrick?' smiled Archie. 'I'd have thought you'd want to stay round here and get her into bed, or summat. I must say you've been showing a lot of interest in her these last few weeks . . .'

'Sandie's not one for wasting time on useless blokes,' Mike said. 'That's summat I've come to realise. She once told me that; she had no time for people who wouldn't work or try to work.'

'What's brought all this about, then?' asked Archie.

'Jackie. Thinking about Jackie and how lucky I was – I mean, Archie, I caused that accident. I got him to stop and wait for me. It could have been me lying in that hospital, I was on the back of the bike, remember. Turner would have hit me if I hadn't got off . . .'

'You can't blame yourself, Mike, for God's sake. It was Turner's fault, I reckon, boozing himself silly and running down a member of the working class like you'd run down a dog.'

'Don't talk rubbish, Archie. We had no lights and we'd parked on the road. Turner saved Jackie's life

126

– and I'm not going to hear anyone say he didn't. Anyway, I've changed my views now, and I reckon you should.'

'Become a capitalist lackey, you mean? Let myself become a member of the oppressed working classes, let myself be used and abused by the forces of capitalism?'

'Archie, you really do talk a lot of rubbish, you know,' said Mike. 'Come on, let's get down to the Woolpack for a pint or two; I'll buy you a pint made by a capitalist brewer and sold in a capitalist pub and I'll use money from my Giro which has been given to me out of taxes earned by capitalist entrepreneurs.'

'You know your trouble, Mike?' said Archie, falling into step by his side.

'No?'

'You have no social conscience, that's what.'

Mike chuckled; now he had made up his mind to leave Beckindale and to seek his fortune elsewhere, it seemed that the worries over his part in Jackie's accident were diminishing. He'd visit Jackie as soon as the hospital allowed it.

Seth Armstrong, deeply upset by Jackie's accident, kept himself busy by organising his outing. The date had been fixed for a fortnight on Saturday and he decided to call on Alan Turner to issue an invitation.

'What is it now, Seth?' Turner was on the telephone when Seth entered and Caroline Bates was working on a thick file of papers, checking it for details of wheat yield over the last five years. 'Can't you see I'm busy?'

127

'Me too, Mr Turner. We're busy folk, you and me. But I allus say that if you want a job doing proper, you give it to a busy person. He'll allus find time, Mr Turner, just as I've found time to come in here to see you on a very important matter.'

'Oh, all right, what is it, Seth?' and he replaced the telephone. 'There's no reply anyway. You'd think Head Office would be able to answer a tele-phone call.'

'The staff outing, Mr Turner,' beamed Seth.

'I'm leaving that in your hands, Seth. Delegation, you know. You are in complete charge of that outing.'

'Aye, well, that's why I'm here, Mr Turner. As the man in charge, you see.'

'If you're in charge, Seth, I fail to see why you are here to seek my advice.'

Caroline Bates had now started to listen to this exchange. It was typical of the frequent battles between Seth and Turner.

'Well, it's summat very important, you see, Mr Turner, and the lads have asked me to come along to see you about it. You know we're going to Cleethorpes, on a surprise outing, Mr Turner?'

'Whereabouts in Cleethorpes?' asked Turner.

'That's the surprise, Mr Turner,' beamed Seth. 'But, as the man in charge of the outing, the others have asked me to come and see you.'

'Oh, for heaven's sake, Seth, get on with it. Do you want me to donate a prize or something? A crate of beer, perhaps, for the sing-along in the bus?'

'Well, I must say that's a very generous idea, Mr

Turner; yes, a crate of beer for the lads would be most welcome.'

'Good, then order one from Amos, and put it on my account. Now, is that all?'

'No, Mr Turner, that wasn't why I'd come, not really.'

'Good God, man, I'm up to the neck in accounts.'

'It was for summat else, Mr Turner.' And now Mrs Bates was having to conceal her smiles behind her hand.

'You want some cash from me, then? From NY? As their official contribution to the outing, is that it?'

'What were you thinking of, Mr Turner?' Seth's moustache bristled in anticipation. 'An official contribution for our meals, happen? Fish-and-chips all round?'

'I was thinking of, say, £50, a donation from NY's entertainment account – for the staff outing.'

'Now that's what I call a real generous gesture, Mr Turner, and I know the lads will drink your health on the trip.'

'See to it, Mrs Bates, will you? Draw the cash today and let Seth have it. Mark it down to "Staff Outing".'

'I know the men will be most grateful, Mr Turner,' added Caroline Bates. 'It'll give them a real day out.'

'I like to think I do show a surprisingly generous streak from time to time,' beamed Turner. 'It is a way of thanking the men for their work during the last months. Now Seth,' he turned to his gamekeeper again. 'Is that all?'

'No, Mr Turner, that wasn't why I came, really. It was for summat else.'

'Look, Seth, I have been very patient with you and I am very busy. So what is it this time? What else are you going to ask me for?'

'Well, Mr Turner,' and Seth stood his ground, 'you remember when you said that leadership come from the top, that all great leaders have an affinity with their men?'

'Did I say that, Seth?'

'Oh, aye, Mr Turner, and I'll tell you summat, it's words like that that mean summat to your work force. Gives 'em a sense of pride, you see.'

'Really? I had no idea,' and Turner began to preen himself. 'So what is it that the men want from me?'

'It's a sacrifice they're asking, Mr Turner,' said Seth. 'The sort of sacrifice only a born leader can make, an act of selflessness that inspires other men, you see . . .'

And at this stage, even Mrs Bates began to wonder what the scheming Seth was plotting.

'Oh, get on with it, Seth.' Even Turner was now suspecting something.

'Well, everybody on the trip, Mr Turner, has asked me to approach you to see if you would like to join us on the bus.'

'Come with you, you mean? To Cleethorpes?'

'Aye, that's it, Mr Turner. It wouldn't be the same without you. Incomplete, the lads said.'

'Really, I had no idea they thought so much about me.'

'Oh, they think a lot about you, Mr Turner.'

'Are you going, Mrs Bates?' Turner asked his secretary.

'No, I can't; Malcolm and I have already booked an appointment with our solicitor, you see . . .'

'Oh, well, I suppose as leader of the NY team in Beckindale that I had better make an appearance. Yes, all right, Seth, I accept with pleasure.'

'Right ho, Mr Turner, t'bus leaves the post office a fortnight on Saturday at ten o'clock prompt. I'll remind you nearer the date, and we've a lunch fixed up so there's no need to fetch sandwiches.'

'Good, then I look forward to it. Make a note in my diary, Mrs Bates.'

And off went Seth, looking very pleased with himself.

When he'd gone, Turner said, 'You know, Mrs Bates, this could be a sign of a new realism among the men. As a rule they don't want the boss anywhere near them on their staff outing, and now they've made a very appealing approach. I'm quite flattered, Mrs Bates, quite moved in fact.'

'I do hope you enjoy the trip, Mr Turner.' She smiled to herself, wondering what Seth had up his sleeve.

In the days that followed, Jackie Merrick's condition remained static. Pat and Jack were allowed short visits twice a day, once in the morning and again each evening, but it was stressed that these must be of a very brief duration. But Jackie quickly came through the worst of his ordeal, thanks to the dedication and skill of the hospital staff, though at first he had no real idea of the seriousness or extent of his injuries. In those early days he was cheerful, and popular with the nurses.

After a week or so, more visitors were allowed; Archie and Mike called, with Archie promising that the Marxist revolution would incarcerate all landowners and especially those who drove Land Rovers and knocked down motor cyclists, while Mike was still convinced that he was, in many ways, responsible for Jackie's condition. Jackie tried to cheer him up by saying it had been pure accident, with the bike's condition being at fault, and with Turner being at fault too for not seeing the bike – after all, it did have a red reflector on the back and that had been functioning quite properly. Alison Caswell called too, but it was more the meeting of a friend than of a lover for she had known some time before this accident that she and Jackie would not continue their romance.

The friendship remained, however, and she did become a regular and welcome visitor for Jackie. Tom called too, often bringing Sandie with him, but he had the sense not to bring Derek Warner – Jackie's memory of poaching with Warner would do nothing to encourage his recovery.

Annie came too, usually being transported by Henry Wilks. Henry was now working on the farm, but he was not finding the work very easy; he was determined to achieve all that Jackie would have done, but he was so much slower. However, he did help with all the tough chores – milking, swilling out the mistle, ploughing, helping Matt with the sheep, walling, cleaning out ditches and a host of other labouring jobs.

The surprise of the week was Tom Merrick's offer to help with the work at Emmerdale Farm. Annie told Jackie about it during one of her visits.

'He's staying at Demdyke till he gets himself sorted out,' she told her grandson. 'I do know he's been in touch with the oil rig in Aberdeen, and there is a possibility of a job. Not the one that he had before he got put in prison, but another one in the same department on-shore. It seems he was a good worker up there, Jackie, and they'd welcome him back. He's got to keep in touch, apparently, and they hope to let him know within a month or so. Anyway, he's offered to lend a hand.'

'That's amazing, Ma,' Jackie beamed. 'It really is. I mean, Tom always said he'd never come near the place, and he's often wished Jack all the harm in the world.'

'Well, he's changed. He wants no money, he says, just his keep, so we'll feed him and we'll let him use Demdyke until he's got a job fixed up.'

'What sort of work is he doing, then?' asked Jackie.

'All the things you used to do,' said Annie. 'He's helping Matt today, they're putting up a lamb shelter and Matt say's Tom's a very good worker and a big help.'

'I'll have to watch myself, then!' laughed Jackie. 'He might do me out of my own job!'

Annie smiled. 'He's really impressed at the way you have settled down to farming,' she said. 'I do know he appreciates what Jack has done for you, showing you the skills you've got, and Tom wants to

133

try and do the same work – just to see whether he likes it an' all!'

'It's good of you to let him stay,' said Jackie.

'He's Sandie's family, Jackie, and she's part of our family, so it's the least we can do. I must say there are some good points to Tom – and this is one of them, helping us out like this – he could have gone straight back to Scotland.'

Annie told him all the gossip in the village, of Amos and his beekeeping, of Seth and the forthcoming staff outing to Cleethorpes and of Sandie's enjoyment of her own work in the auction mart.

The one subject she did not discuss was Jack's affair, she still had no idea whether Jackie had ever known of this. Annie knew that Jackie had been oblivious of the tension between Pat and Jack because, at its height, he had been too involved with Alison and his thoughts of marriage to her. The fact that he was living at Demdyke Cottage during the worst of that crisis had sheltered him from the knowledge that his father was having a passionate affair with a younger woman, and that his mother was going through yet another miserable time in her life.

They chatted about the lambing time that was now in full swing and Annie did take the opportunity to refer to Alison.

'She's been to see me,' beamed Jackie. 'She brought me some magazines and books.'

'You won't ignore the lass, will you?' asked Annie. 'She would be good for you, Jackie, now and in the future.'

'There's no romance now, Ma, you know,' he told

her. 'No likely wedding. We're friends, sure, but nowt else.'

This merely confirmed Annie's guesses, but to hear Jackie say it brought a sense of disappointment; she had long considered that Alison would make a very welcome addition to the Emmerdale family. But she put that possibility to the back of her mind as she realised that her priority was to do all in her power to ensure that Jackie was nursed back to full health.

For Jack and Pat, things did appear to be improving, if only slowly. Pat still found it difficult to trust Jack, and from time to time she did wonder if he and Karen were meeting again. There had been occasions when he seemed to be thinking of her, times when he'd been watching television, for example, and had not been following the programme; times in the mistle when he'd not talked to her but instead had been gazing into space, his mind a thousand miles away from the task in hand. In bed, he had had several very unsettled nights. She knew he was going through a very difficult time. But Jack would not talk; she did her best to persuade him to discuss his worries, even if it meant talking about Karen, but he kept all his thoughts deep within his own mind. This hurt Pat, but she knew she must accept it as part of Jack's character. At least she had felt she could allow him to return to her bedroom.

Pat did her best not to nag at Jack, not to pressure him into talking when clearly he did not wish to, and yet she was worried about his silence. And then one evening, when Annie had been taken into Hotten by

135

Henry to visit Jackie, and when Sandie was having another evening out with Mike West, Pat suddenly realised Jack was missing.

He had been in the implement shed, working on a tractor, when one of the huge mudguards had become loose, and she took a cup of coffee out to him. But he was no longer there. She called his name several times around the buildings, searching the mistle, the new sheep shelter, the barns and other places, including Grandad's workshop, but there was no sign of Jack.

With a sinking heart, she returned to the farm kitchen, still bearing his mug of coffee. Had he suddenly gone to visit Karen? Had she been on his mind all this time? In the absence of any other explanation, the secrecy worried her; the sudden disappearance had all the hallmarks of an illicit visit to Karen. She put the coffee on the table and stood alone, lost in worrying thoughts, full of disappointment and sorrow. And then she heard a noise from upstairs, from their bedroom.

'Jack?' She did not shout the name, but simply uttered it to herself. 'Jack, is that you?'

She climbed the stairs now, heart thumping and saw the bedroom light was glowing under the door. She opened it carefully. Jack was sitting on the bed, and it was clear from where she stood, that he had been weeping.

'Jack,' she went to him and slipped an arm around his shoulders. 'Jack, luv, what is it?'

Now she settled at his side, her arm about him as he roughly brushed away the tears in his eyes.

'Sorry,' he said, hugging her.

They remained locked in each other's arms for a few minutes and said nothing. Pat knew she must allow Jack to say what he wanted in his own time.

'I'm sorry,' he said at length. 'Sorry, Pat, for everything.'

She did not respond in words, but held him tightly. After a long pause, he added, 'I don't know how you can bear to be with me, Pat, to touch me even, after what I've done.'

'Darling, don't, it's all over . . .'

'No, it's not all over. Look at Jackie. If ever anyone needed a loving family, it's him. And look what I almost did, out of selfishness, stupidity. I could never have forgiven myself if this had happened and I'd not been around, not been here . . . I came so close, Pat, so close to ruining everything.'

'Hey, this is not like you.' She kissed his wet cheek. 'Jackie's going to pull through now, the doctors are pleased with his progress.'

'He called me Dad this morning,' said Jack. 'He acknowledged me as his real father . . .'

'He needs us now, Jack,'

'I know, I know just how much he needs us, both of us. I suddenly realized how much I had almost thrown away, Pat. You know, you've been the strong one – how you could continue to love me for what I've done to you . . .'

'But I do, Jack, I do love you. That gave me strength to go on, to bring you home that night.'

'You were wonderful . . .'

'I couldn't live without you, Jack, I had to bring you home, just as I can't live without Jackie, either. He needs us now, both of us, because he's going to go through one hell of a tough time. And he is our son, yours and mine.'

'We'll never let him down,' said Jack, kissing her fondly. 'You know, I do love you, Pat, and I'll never hurt you again as long as I live. I want us to be happy, all of us, as a real family unit.'

'So do I,' she whispered, tears of relief pouring down her cheeks.

Chapter Eight

Jackie lay in hospital with his left leg encased in plaster and his lower body immobile as his fractured bones began to knit. As he grew stronger with the passing weeks, it seemed to the occupants of Emmerdale Farm that the worst of the year was over. Annie, having presided over the family and its terrible sequence of problems, felt that an improvement was in the air, and that something better must replace the traumas which had bedevilled the family since last autumn.

On a sunny afternoon, she walked around the farm and its fields, admiring the newest of lambs, the cries of the geese and the hens with their broods of new chicks. Even the sheep, known for their stupidity, were teaching their lambs how to cope with life in the open air, how to scent danger and how to find shelter against the chill winds that blew from the Pennines. The hens were doing likewise, teaching the tiny chicks how to scratch for tasty titbits among the roots of the grass or in the dust of the farmyard. And in the hedgerows and copses around Emmerdale, the wild creatures were bringing their latest broods into the troubled world. Young rabbits abounded to become prey to young foxes and stoats, while the birds of the hedgerows produced their broods of tiny fledglings only a small percentage of which would reach maturity.

As Annie walked, the exercise eased her increasingly painful rheumatism, if only temporarily, but it allowed her to reflect upon nature's ways. She wondered whether the animals managed their relationships better than the human race. Some wildlife did mate for life, such as wild swans, kittiwakes and gannets, as well as greylag geese and even jackdaws. Annie knew that if a greylag goose lost its partner through death, it would never seek another; it remained faithful to that first partner. She drew comparisons between nature and her own troubled family.

She also wondered whether she had done her best for Grandad, whether Jack and Pat would completely salvage their marriage, whether Joe would always live in France, whether Jackie would ever walk again and whether Sandie would settle in Beckindale. Sandie was seeing a lot of Mike West, though she stressed there was no romance; she did not particularly like Mike in that way, but went out with him for companionship.

To add to Jack's trouble at the this time, it had been discovered that the Emmerdale Friesians were producing too much milk; the new EEC quotas stipulated how much could be produced by each dairy farmer and Emmerdale had been told to reduce their output – the penalty would be a massive fine, something which the farm could not afford.

And yet, if it reduced its quantity of milk, there would be a corresponding reduction in income . . . it was a problem Jack would have to solve. Annie knew it was troubling him for he hated formalities and red-tape. The only acceptable solution was the sale of some cows. He disliked that idea because it had taken him many years, with a lot of effort, a lot of cash and indeed a great deal of resistance from others, before he'd been able to build the herd to its present level, but there seemed no alternative. Annie recalled his misery last night when he'd finally made up his mind.

'They'll have to go, Ma; half a dozen at least. It breaks my heart – we never had this kind of trouble before we joined the Common Market. Mind, we could do with an injection of cash right now – a lot of our machinery is getting antique, and we could do with renewing that tractor . . . it really is getting to the stage where the muck is holding it together. Matt might have to sell a few sheep an' all, if we have to raise more cash.'

'That won't suit him,' she'd said. 'It's not been the easiest of lambing seasons, has it? And with Jackie out of commission, poor Matt's been working flat out, taking on too much. Tom's been a help and so has Henry, but Matt's had to tell them everything that needed doing, then check their work when they've done it. It's hard on Matt.'

It was while she was alone with her thoughts, that Annie noticed Dolly heading towards her. She looked very cheerful as she strode up the slope of the field behind the farm.

'Hi, Ma, I saw you walking up here. Nowt wrong, is there?'

'No, lass. Nowt's wrong. I'm just airing my old bones and thinking about my family, about it being such a terrible few months. I reckon things can only get better.'

'You've got to look at life like that, Ma,' said Dolly. 'But when I saw you, I thought I'd pass on our bit of news.'

'Oh?' Annie's eyes brightened. 'Good news, is it?'

'Mebbe soon,' Dolly told her, walking at her side. 'Me and Matt have decided to try for another bairn, a sister or a brother for Sam.'

'Oh, well, that would be nice.' Annie meant every word.

Dolly explained how Jackie's accident had made them consider their own future, and Sam's future, and then she said, 'We have tried before, Ma, but nothing's happened, so I went to the specialist in Hotten. He gave me a good examination and said there's no reason why I can't have another child. Matt went an' all – he took a bit of persuading, I might add – but he's OK too. So we're going to really try for a baby now. I thought you'd like to know.'

'That's the best news I've heard this year!' Annie smiled ruefully. 'It has been a time of doom and gloom, hasn't it? So this is marvellous. Matt's in full agreement, is he?'

'Yes,' Dolly beamed. 'I think he was a bit uncertain before Jackie's accident, but now he's completely in favour.'

'Jackie's troubles have caused a lot of folk to think deeply,' Annie told her. 'It's funny how good can come out of the worst troubles, isn't it?' They walked in silence for a while.

'Jack and Pat seem to have settled their differences now, eh?' Dolly said finally.

142

'Aye, I think they have. They're very much together now, Dolly, they go everywhere with each other. Jack knows what a fool he has been – it was Jackie that brought them back together again – I mean really together. It made Jack realise he'd got a lot here, with Jackie and Pat. They're one happy family now – even Jackie can see that. He completely accepts Jack as his real dad now. Jack's taking Pat away for a weekend soon, by the way, the minute they can trust Tom and Henry with the milking!'

'Tom's been helping Matt,' Dolly said. 'I think they get on very well.'

'It's given him a good appetite if nothing else,' smiled Annie. 'But he's told Pat and Jack that he'll stay to make sure they can have a break, then he'll go back to Aberdeen. The oil company has said there is a job for him.'

'So things are brightening up, Ma?'

'I hope so, Dolly, I really hope so.'

But for one woman, the gloom and despair had not lifted; in fact, it had deepened. Caroline Bates dragged herself to work after a terrible meeting with her solicitor; she had been told that her husband wished to divorce her and that she must leave the family home in Hotten. There would be a share-out of the contents and the financial arrangements would be completed in due course, but in the meantime, she faced a bleak and uncertain future. Until now, she had managed to conceal much of her distress, but it was with a heavy heart that she sat at her desk, tears streaming down her face. She was like that when Alan Turner came into the office, and at first, he did not notice her tears.

'Well, Mrs Bates,' he began, rubbing his hands as he faced the day. 'What have we this morning? More statistics to compile for head office . . . ? Oh, I say, I'm sorry.'

She was trying to wipe her eyes and hoped he had not noticed her appearance.

'It's all right, Mr Turner,' she sniffed. 'I'll be all right in a minute.'

'Mrs Bates, er, Caroline, can I help? I mean, would it be any use talking to me . . . you could always take the morning off, the day off, even, if it would help.'

'No, I'd rather stay at work, Mr Turner, I need to be kept busy.'

'Yes, well, just as you wish. I'd like to help if I could.'

She shook her head and blew her nose. 'It's Malcolm,' and now she burst into a flood of tears. 'He's leaving me and wants a divorce. He's got another woman, Mr Turner, a younger one, Sonia somebody or other, and they want to get married. I'm in the way . . . I said I'll divorce him . . .'

'Is that why you are seeing your solicitor on Saturday?'

'Yes, when we arranged that we were talking of a separation, not a divorce; we thought if we separated for a while, as an experiment, then maybe we could work something out. But now . . . There's the children too, Nick and Kathy, and he wants to sell the house . . .'

'Look, Mrs Bates, I know what you are going

144

through and if my own experience can be of any help, any help at all, then all you have to do is ask.'

'Thank you, Mr Turner, that is kind . . . I just don't know what I'm going to do at the moment, I can't think straight, let alone plan for the future.'

'Well, there is one positive thing I can do even at this stage, Mrs Bates.' He had suddenly realised that he might be of assistance to her. 'I know it might be rather early to suggest this, but, well, chances like this don't come every day.'

'Chances, Mr Turner?' she looked at him, calmer now as she dried her eyes.

'Yes, a house, Mrs Bates. If you need a house, there's that cottage in the village. You'll know it, it's almost opposite the Woolpack. It needs some attention – a good clean-out and some decorating – but the fabric is sound. It has a good roof, three bedrooms, modern bathroom, a nice kitchen, dining room, lounge and small garden. The rent, for a member of staff, would be very reasonable.'

She knew the cottage he meant; it was very pleasant.

'You mean that, Mr Turner?'

'Yes, of course I do. It's empty now – in fact, it was made empty before you came to work here, and NY couldn't decide what to do with it. Our staff tend to buy their own properties now. So if you need somewhere to live, then I could recommend to Head Office that you should become the tenant. There is no one else in line for it just now, Mrs Bates, and if we can't find a tenant, then NY might decide to sell it. We'd lose it for ever then. Have a look around it whenever you want.'

145

'I don't know how to thank you, Mr Turner. This could solve a rather immediate problem . . . I would like to move out of Malcolm's house just as soon as possible, you understand it's not easy living under the same roof . . .'

'Then say no more. I will get our men to give it a thorough cleaning and then we'll decorate it,' and he picked up the telephone to call Jock, Bill and Seth into the office. 'And because it's NY property, NY will foot the bill!'

'I don't know how to thank you, Mr Turner,' she said again.

'Nonsense,' he said. 'It's nice to be able to help someone. So shall we say it's agreed? With the rent to be determined at staff rates?'

And she smiled her happiness.

'Good. Well, what about some work? How do you feel about that?'

'Ready, just as soon as you are, Mr Turner.'

Meanwhile, some other members of NY staff had important matters on their minds. That lunchtime, over their pints in the Woolpack, Bill and Seth discussed the final plans for the NY Estates staff outing. Seth told him that the bus had been arranged and it would depart at 10am as agreed.

'So, how many's going?' asked Bill. 'Have we a good turnout?'

'Eight,' smiled Seth.

'Eight?' cried Bill. 'But I thought we usually had thirty or forty, what with wives, families and friends.'

'A lot didn't fancy going to Cleethorpes,' said

Seth. 'I think I put 'em off when I said you couldn't see t'sea when t'tide was out. But we do have four full domino teams, Bill.'

'Domino teams?'

'Aye, eight of us, eight blokes. Now, I happen to know there's a prize domino competition going on, you see, with a lawnmower for t'best individual score in the competition, and good prizes for teams. Now, as you know, us NY lads are good at dominoes, all that practice we get when Turner's not around . . .'

On the day of the NY Estates staff outing to Cleethorpes, a very battered and noisy coach eased to a halt outside the post office in Beckindale. It was a mini-coach of considerable age and the driver wore greasy brown overalls and large, black boots.

Seth was there to greet him. 'Now then, Sid. You got here, then?'

'Aye, nobbut just. She's not very clever on t'hills, Seth, and when she gets a load aboard, she'll have a job climbing over a cattle grid. But she's just right for you, she'll never get up Mealy Mires Bank, just like you wanted . . .'

'Not a word about that!' hissed Seth. 'Our boss is coming with us, so when this old crate conks, we'll have to make a go of getting her up that hill.'

'Aye, I know about all that,' said Sid.

'Right, now the pub's just over t'brow – the Spotted Calf – and I've seen them about fixing fish-and-chips for us all, with free booze and food for you, for your co-operation.'

'Do they all know we're not going to Cleethorpes, then?'

'Quiet, don't breathe a word,' said Seth. 'You're getting paid for going to Cleethorpes, paid in advance due to my clever planning . . . right?'

'I understand. Ah, this must be your boss, eh?'

Alan Turner was striding purposefully towards the coach and the nearer he got, the less enthusiastic was his smile.

'Morning, Mr Turner,' smiled Seth. 'All set then?'

'I thought there'd have been more here by now, Seth, you know, wives and families, children, staff from the Estate.'

'Aye, they'll be here soon, Mr Turner. Now I'd best collect that crate o' beer you donated. Amos'll have it ready.'

As Seth stalked off to secure the beer, Turner turned to Sid and said, 'You're our driver, are you?'

'Driver, conductor, mechanic, owner, repairer. Sid Thompson of Thompson's Luxury Touring Coaches,' replied Sid with pride.

'And this will be the reserve vehicle, eh? For the overflow?' beamed Turner.

'No, this is my only bus. I've only got this one, mister. There's only eight of you going on this trip, so you wouldn't need a fifty-seven seater or summat as big as that.'

'Eight?' growled Turner, looking in vain for Seth. He stomped up and down, wondering whether this was the truth, and then Seth staggered out of the Woolpack with a crate of beer. Sid opened the rear emergency door of the old bus and Seth slid the crate inside.

'Good of you to donate that beer, Mr Turner, the act of a gentleman.'

148

'Seth, this, er, gentleman, tells me there's only eight of us going on this trip. I thought it was a full-scale outing for workers and their families . . .'

'Aye, well it was, Mr Turner, but most of 'em wanted to go to Scarborough or Bridlington in the summer, so when they found out we were going to Cleethorpes now, they didn't want to come. But a promise is a promise, as you know, and so we felt that those who wanted to go, should go. And we're right glad you could make it.'

By now, Bill Middleton and Jock MacDonald were coming across the street, followed by four other Estate workers.

'Well, Sid, we're all here now,' beamed Seth. 'All aboard, lads, and the beer's in the back.'

Alan Turner groaned aloud as he mounted the steps. As the creaking old bus rumbled out of Beckindale, he began to ask himself how on earth he had been tricked into agreeing to this jaunt. He thought a working men's club in Cleethorpes was the last place he'd find enjoyment. He sank into his seat although he did accept a bottle of beer.

'Cheers, Mr Turner,' and everyone raised their bottles to the boss.

But within an hour of leaving Beckindale, Turner realised that the old bus would never reach Clee-thorpes. It coughed and jerked as it attempted any incline and the men inside joked and laughed as Sid somehow coaxed it over successive summits. But the end came on Mealy Mires Bank. With a gallant cough, a leap forward and an awful groaning of brakes, gears and wheels, the old coach came to a halt.

'We'll have to push her up the rest of it,' said Seth. 'Right, lads, everybody out and shoulders to the wheel.'

With no more ado, the eight NY men, Alan Turner included, climbed out of the bus and began to push; Sid engaged bottom gear and very, very slowly, the old coach climbed the hill. After many minutes of effort and perspiration, the old bus reached the summit and promptly coughed its last.

'She's fizzled out all together,' said Sid. 'Not a spark of life in her at all, gents.'

'We can freewheel down t'other side,' Seth pointed along the road. 'See, there's a village down there, a mile away.'

'So there is!' smiled the perspiring Turner. 'Maybe you can get this thing fixed there, er, Sid.'

And so they all climbed aboard and Sid released the brakes. The old coach began to roll forward as it started its descent of the long, sloping hill into Shutterdale.

Seth was standing beside the driver, and he suddenly shouted, 'Hey, Sid, look. There's a pub with a big car park – just down there on t'right. You could pull her in there and we could have a drink or two, or mebbe a game of dominoes or summat, while you get your bus fixed.'

'Good idea,' said Sid in a well-rehearsed response. 'I'll turn her in there.'

And so the NY Estates Staff Outing found themselves in the car park of the Spotted Cow, Shutterdale. It was packed with cars, but there was a convenient place for the bus to ease to a halt without using its engine.

150

'How long'll it take to get your bus fixed?' asked Turner.

'Dunno,' smiled Sid. 'Long enough for your lads to have a pint or two, I'd say.'

'Look, lads,' beamed Seth pointing to a notice as they approached the door of the pub. 'Bar snacks, meals in baskets, and an open domino challenge competition with good prizes. All welcome, it says.'

'It might be better than Cleethorpes,' said Jock MacDonald.

'Just what I was thinking,' said Seth, striding in with Alan Turner on his heels.

'You know, Seth, if that bus had not broken down, I'd have said you had planned all this, but I don't think that even you could arrange for a bus to break down at the very pub that's running a domino competition – with NY providing enough men for several full teams . . .'

'And a lawnmower for the best individual score of the day, Mr Turner. Now, you allus say I should keep my lawn well trimmed . . .'

'Seth!' Turner halted in his tracks. 'Seth, would this bus really have got us all the way to Cleethorpes and back again?'

'That's the surprise, Mr Turner,' chuckled Seth, leading his boss and his team inside.

The NY team, fortified with lots of beer obtained at the Spotted Cow, won the team event and with it the prize of a crate of beer and an inscribed tankard for each member. Seth Armstrong won the individual event and the chairman rose to his feet amid loud cheers to announce the fact, and to inform Seth that he had won the lawnmower. It was awaiting in a paddock at the rear of the inn and even Alan Turner, himself filled with a superb fish-and-chip lunch and well lubricated with whisky and beer, slapped Seth on the back and congratulated him. At the conclusion of the event, everyone trooped to the rear of the pub for the formal presentation.

They gathered in a small, well-shorn paddock where the only inhabitant was a donkey and the chairman said, 'Well, gentlemen – and lady – this is the climax of our day's dominoing. It has been a record event with more teams than ever taking part and there was a surprise when unexpected competitors came from Beckindale in North Yorkshire.

'Now those lads certainly knew how to play dominoes and even though the NY Estate crowd beat us, it gives me great pleasure to award the supreme prize to Mr Seth Armstrong. He has travelled all the way from Beckindale to win the top prize. Mr Armstrong – congratulations. I hope you feel your journey was worthwhile.'

He shook Seth's hand. Seth beamed with pleasure at the audience before peering around to view his prize lawnmower. But the chairman went to the donkey and took its bridle.

'Here we are, one prize lawnmower. Her name is Jessie.'

Seth looked around in embarrassment, thinking this was a sick joke perpetrated by the beaten Spotted Cow team, but the chairman thrust the halter into his hands.

'She loves lawns,' he said confidentially. 'And dahlias, chrysanthemums, lettuces, cabbages . . .'

It was a long time before Seth would believe that this was indeed his prize lawnmower and he was told he must remove it immediately because the paddock in which it lived had been sold.

Following an animated discussion with Sid Thompson, who insisted that Seth purchase a brush and shovel before leaving for home, it was decided that the donkey could travel in the aisle of Sid's bus. And so, after much heaving and pushing up a narrow plank, Jessie was placed in the rear of the bus facing the driver, and tethered to the back of one of the seats. Turner was chuckling the whole time. The entire Beckindale entourage had had a marvellous day out.

'You know, Seth,' said Alan Turner, as the bus, now miraculously repaired, began its slow journey home. 'This is the best day out I've had in years. Most amusing and very relaxing, away from the cares of office. Thank you for inviting me – I wonder if Cleethorpes missed us?'

'Mebbe we should go there now, Mr Turner?' suggested Seth. 'Then I could sell this donkey, it'd be fine on that beach, tha knaws . . .' But everyone booed this proposal.

'I'll keep her on my allotment, then,' conceded Seth.

'It'll be company for Amos's bees,' grinned Bill.

Chapter Nine

During the weeks that followed, Jackie Merrick continued to improve. He found the task of having to lie utterly motionless a most boring and frustrating experience, and his plaster-encased body itched and ached without respite. He was totally dependent upon others for his every need – washing, going to the toilet, dressing – although he could struggle to feed himself, not the cleanest of tasks when lying down. His hands and arms were not affected, but he could not move from his bed, so when the nurses wanted to change his sheets, he had to be lifted out. And when he wanted to visit the toilet, he had to call for help.

When his visitors called, he found he had little to discuss with them, except the events of his long, boring day in the ward and some of the trials of the other patients. He enjoyed Tom Merrick's visits because Tom always livened up the ward with his outrageous behaviour, such as playing marbles with the grapes or telling bawdy jokes so that everyone cried with laughing.

Some of the patients were in a far worse condition than Jackie; he learned that one lad called Stephen would never walk again, such was the extent of his injuries. He too had been involved in a shocking motor cycle accident and it was only after some weeks in hospital that Jackie learned Stephen's younger brother had been killed in the accident. And worse still, Stephen's parents were blaming Stephen for that death. To add to his agony, they had refused to visit him in hospital.

Jackie befriended the unhappy Stephen, who was about Jackie's own age, and made sure that he shared all his presents of fruit, sweets, drinks and magazines with him. He then discovered that Stephen had no idea that he would never walk again. It was Stephen's awful predicament that made Jackie determined not to be defeated; he made a vow that he would walk again and that he would soon be back on the farm, tending his sheep, walking the fells and helping with the multitude of tasks that always needed doing. But it was such a slow process and so painful.

When Henry Wilks and Annie came to visit him one afternoon, they found him depressed and almost in tears. Earlier that day, he had tried to sit in a chair beside the bed. Helped by two strong male nurses, he had scorned them at first, saying that anyone could sit in a chair – but he had not succeeded. Even with their help, he had been unable to achieve that simple task. The pain, his sheer inability to control or manage his movements, and the depressing weakness that resulted from lying in bed for weeks, had all conspired to defeat him. He was still worrying about this when Annie and Henry arrived. He told them of his trials, of the utter hopelessness of trying to do ordinary things and of his misery at being unable to leave.

'I've had enough,' he told them through a mist of tears. 'I really have. I just don't seem to be getting

155

any better – I mean, there's other folks been in here and gone, but I'm still here and all they say is that I'm improving. Look, I'm still in plaster and I still can't even sit in a chair. I mean, how long is it going to take to be normal again? I just want to come home . . .'

Annie stroked his head. 'You are getting better, Jackie.'

'I wish I could believe it, sometimes I think they're not telling me the truth. Look at poor Stephen – he doesn't know he won't walk again, they haven't told him. So why should they tell me?'

Henry spoke with confidence. 'Jackie, your injuries are nowt like as bad as Stephen's. Not in the same league – you have a fractured pelvis which is mending nicely. A major repair like that can't be rushed, it would be foolish to try and hurry it because you'd do damage to yourself and then you'd be right back where you started. But it will mend, in time.'

Jackie slumped back on his pillow and sighed deeply. 'Aye, I know, Henry, but it's just so bloody hard . . . Anyway, how's things back at Emmerdale? I do miss the old spot, you know.'

'Well, there is a bit of news,' Annie smiled. 'Dolly's going to help out at the Woolpack. With Henry working at Emmerdale, and Amos getting busier as the tourists start to come, he needs help. So Dolly's going to work there, several nights a week and some lunchtimes.'

'Dolly? Work in the pub?' laughed Jackie.

'She used to work there, you know. When she

first came to Beckindale. Miss Acaster she was then. You'll remember her coming, Henry?'

'I do,' he smiled. 'She was sent to the Woolpack on a brewery training scheme, to learn about running a pub. And Amos liked her – he was a bit wary at first, mind, but he soon took to her. And she stayed quite a while. Then she met Matt.'

'Well, I never knew that,' smiled Jackie. 'You know, that has cheered me up. I'll try and get out of here especially to order a pint from Dolly. It's summat to work for.'

'That's the spirit, Jackie lad,' said Wilks. 'You sound better already. Oh, and there is another bit of news – about your pal Seth and his NY staff trip to Cleethorpes.'

And so Henry related the saga of Seth's donkey. He told how it had taken to following Alan Turner around the village whenever it could, for it had learned to escape from Seth's allotment by pushing up the sneck of the gate. It seemed Turner had given it a toffee on the bus and it had promptly fallen in love with him. So everywhere that Turner went, the donkey was sure to go. It had also upset Amos because it loved his bees too; it seemed the buzzing from the hive attracted the donkey, who loved to nuzzle it, wobbling it so that the bees buzzed all the more, which in turn made the donkey even happier.

Amos was angry and invoked the allotment rules by saying livestock was not to be kept there, but Seth just ignored him because he maintained Amos's bees were also livestock – and there were many more of them.

And so there was an impasse between the two protagonists, with the donkey roaming the village almost at will, eating flowers, trying to follow Turner into the Woolpack and invading the post office-cum-shop where it could smell toffees. No one quite knew what to do about it, least of all Seth, who found that his plans to make himself popular in the election battle for Presidency of Beckindale Allotments and Horticultural Society had backfired somewhat. Not only had Jessie eaten the long grass from Seth's allotment, she had also eaten lots of vegetables and flowers growing in other allotments so that few would now vote for Seth. Amos, on the other hand, had been delighted at this development and had promptly upgraded his own election campaign by blaming Seth for the range of destruction and disasters on the allotments.

Henry told a good story and by the time this visit was over, Jackie had cheered up a good deal.

But the presence of Henry and Annie made him even more determined to walk. He decided to try by himself. An opportunity presented itself that evening as the sister was busy in her office. Jackie wanted to go to the toilet which was located at the far end of his ward.

He had been taken there several times and now felt he could, with the aid of his crutches and some support from the bed ends en route, make that journey. And so he crept out of bed, slipped the crutches under his armpits and began the trip. It was hard work, but he arrived. He got inside the cubicle, and then disaster happened. His good leg simply would not stand the strain; his weakened muscles and lack of control meant that he collapsed inside the door.

'Nurse,' he sobbed. 'Nurse, help me, please . . .'

He could not get back onto his feet and found himself panicking as the reality of the situation impressed itself upon him. 'Nurse . . .'

A beautiful Asian nurse rushed in, assessed the situation in an instant and called for help. A second nurse helped her lift him back onto his feet and they supported him, guiding him back to his bed. By this time, Sister Henshaw was waiting for him, standing beside his bed with her arms folded and a very severe expression on her face.

'Nurse Sharma, Nurse Peters, what is the meaning of this?'

Jackie suddenly realised that they were going to be blamed for his mishap, and he said, 'It was me, Sister, not them. I got out of bed, to go to the loo . . . it's not their fault.'

She ignored his plea on their behalf and ticked them off by saying, 'Patients should not be left unattended if they are liable to be a risk to themselves. And you, young man, should not have been so silly.'

'I couldn't wait . . .' he began.

'Then you'll have to learn to wait,' she snapped. 'You could do yourself irreparable harm by frolicking about like that. Now get to bed and stay there, and don't you dare move until assistance is available.'

'No, Sister,' he replied meekly.

When she had gone, Nurse Sharma tucked him in and said, 'Look, if you need help, all you have to do is ring your bell.'

'I know all about that,' he snapped. 'I've been

159

ringing my bell for weeks, getting folks to help me do this and do that, so I thought I'd try to do something for myself . . .'

'Well, it wasn't a very good idea, was it?' She was smiling at him now. 'But no harm done, fortunately.'

'You new then?' He tried to be chatty now that the fearsome Sister Henshaw had vanished; Nurse Peters was attending to another man further along the ward.

'New to this ward but not new to the hospital,' Nurse Sharma told him. 'I was in geriatrics before I came here, and in the childrens' ward before that. They move us around to get experience. Now I've got you rebellious lot to cope with!'

'From India, are you?' smiled Jackie, looking at her beautiful dark skin and eyes.

'No, Hotten,' she grinned. 'I'm British, just like you. My dad's a doctor in Hotten . . .'

'No offence meant!' he said. 'I just wondered if you'd been sent here for, well, training.'

'No offence taken,' she smiled at him. 'But look, er . . .'

'Jackie,' he said as she examined the board at the foot of his bed to discover his name. 'Jackie Merrick.'

'Jackie. Look, I know you feel helpless and that you want to get back to normal, but that trip you tried just now was very silly, very silly indeed. That fall could have undone the work of many weeks, and you could have had to start all over again – that pelvis of yours is not mended yet, you know. It'll take a lot more time and a lot more patience.'

'I know, I'm sorry. It was just that I wanted to do

something for myself. I didn't meant to get you and Nurse Peters into trouble.'

'If it's nothing worse than that, there's not a lot to worry about. Now, you behave yourself and the sooner you learn to do as you're told, the sooner you'll get home.'

He lay back and sighed. 'It's nice to see a new face on this ward,' he said. 'God, I'm tired. What's your name?'

'Sharma,' she said. 'Nurse Sharma.'

'No, your Christian name,' he continued.

'I'm not a Christian,' she told him without any malice. 'You mean my forename?'

'Oh, aye, well, yes.'

'Sita,' she said somewhat coyly.

'That's nice,' and he relaxed now, easing himself into his bed and yawning. 'You'll be looking after me for a while, then?'

'Until they move me to another ward,' she smiled.

'That's nice,' said Jackie dreamily. 'Really nice . . . I'm looking forward to being here now . . . I really am . . .' and his words were lost as he drifted into a heavy sleep, exhausted by his efforts. She tucked him into his bed and smiled upon him. It was good to have patients with a bit of character.

Meanwhile, there was a great deal of excitement in the Skilbeck household. Matt, weary after a tough spell of lambing, came home to find a rather special meal on the table.

'Hello, luv, what's this?' he beamed, wondering if he had forgotten an anniversay, a birthday or some other special occasion. But Dolly told him she had

161

some very important news and she wanted to tell him during his favourite meal when he was relaxed and happy.

'You've got a pay rise at the Woolpack?' he started to guess at the reason, but she shook her head. She made him go upstairs to get bathed and changed. Young Sam was already in bed, having been taken upstairs early with his favourite bedtime story and as Matt washed and shaved, Dolly busied herself with the dinner. She fussed over his steak, making sure the starter was just right, and opened a bottle of red wine to be ready on the table. Matt took his time, puzzling over these celebrations by Dolly and eventually he returned, smelling of shampoo and cleanliness.

She passed him a glass of his favourite malt whisky and settled him down on the settee as she poured herself a dry sherry. 'So,' he said. 'You've won the premium bonds? You've been awarded a prize hairdo in a woman's magazine? Won the Spot the Ball competition?'

She shook her head, enjoying his attempts to discover a reason, and then, when he had exhausted all his guesses, she said, 'You do know, Matt. You must! We've been trying for so long and, well, I went to the doctor's this morning . . . and it's positive.'

'Pregnant, you mean?' he gasped. 'You mean you're pregnant?'

'Aye,' and happiness radiated from her face. 'Definitely; I was unsure a month ago, so I said nowt, and then this time, well, there is no doubt. I'm a good two months on, Matt . . .'

162

'I don't know what to say!'

She kissed him tenderly. 'Don't say anything, there's no need. I can see the happiness in your eyes. Oh, Matt, this is wonderful news . . . I'm so happy.'

'Hadn't you better start taking things easy?' He suddenly showed signs of worry. 'I mean, this extra work at the Woolpack, and some of those farming jobs, helping me with the lambs. That's heavy work, luv, and this sherry . . .'

'It's all right!' she smiled. 'I've been told by the doctor what I can do and what I can't. And I am a grown woman, you know. I'm all right working at the Woolpack for a while yet, and Amos or Henry always carries the bottles up from the cellar.'

Both before the meal and during it, they chattered like a newly married couple, making plans and discussing their future with emphasis on how Sam should be told, how he might respond, when was the right time to tell Annie, Pat and Jack, as well as Jackie and Sandie, whether they wanted a boy or a girl, what names they should be considering. They talked late into the evening with Matt telling her he would wash up while she put her feet up with a coffee.

They decided that the family should be told as soon as possible, leaving Dolly to inform Annie and Pat, who would tell the others, although Matt felt he wanted to tell Jack. With Tom and Henry responsible for milking, he and Jack were due to work on the fells tomorrow, checking the latest arrivals among the lambs and so Matt would pass on the good news.

163

Annie was the first to be told, with Dolly taking immense care to ensure that no one knew before her. And Annie was delighted, knowing that a happy family was a recipe for success in life. She knew that young Sam needed a brother or a sister, and Dolly received a similarly happy response from Pat.

There were hugs and kisses all round after which Annie brewed a cup of tea as the three of them sat down to chatter about the news. As the three women talked, Dolly wondered if Matt had managed to tell Jack.

High on the fells, Matt and Jack settled down for their mid-morning break, known in Yorkshire as 'lowance time. Owing to them working so far from the farmhouse, they had taken flasks of coffee and some cakes with them, and now enjoyed the welcome break. The wind was chilly as it whipped across the Pennines and along the exposed slopes of the fells and dales to sting their cheeks and bring tears to their eyes. But the little lambs seemed to be flourishing, for although the number of births had not been particularly high this season, the losses had been low.

'Seems like we've bred some good stock this time,' said Matt, warming to his subject. 'Few losses, good sturdy lambs.'

'They look well enough to me,' said Jack. 'Quality instead of quantity this year, eh?'

'Aye,' smiled Matt. 'Quality instead of quantity. Nice way of putting it, Jack. How's things with you now – and Pat?

'Couldn't be better, Matt. I was a bloody fool, I know that now, and I didn't realise the hurt I was causing. But, well, Jackie's accident brought me to my senses. It's a tough way of bringing old fools like me back to reality, but it worked.

'You know, Matt, until his accident, I had no idea of the riches I've got here, all around me. The farm, a family, good friends, lovely countryside . . . what more can a fellow want? And there go I, behaving like a love-sick teenager and threatening to destroy it all, for myself and others. Anyway, Matt, it's all over. I do keep bumping into Karen when I'm at the Mart, but there's no danger now – she knows that, an' all.'

'Aye, well, I reckon Jackie's trouble's done us all some good, Jack. Made us look hard at our own lives, me and Dolly an' all.'

'You've been sneaking off, Matt?' laughed Jack. 'Having a passionate liaison in Connelton or some-where equally exotic?'

'Nay, don't be daft, Jack. I'm not like that.'

'I thought I wasn't.'

'Anyroad, Jack, as I was saying, me and Dolly have been thinking. About Jackie, about how awful if he'd, well, died. Got crippled for life. Summat awful like that. And it got us thinking that if summat ever happened to young Sam . . .'

'I know what you're saying, Matt. You could lose everything, everyone, through just one stupid action.'

'Aye, so that's why me and Dolly decided we'd try to increase our family, Jack.'

'You're not saying you want a bigger cottage and a pay rise, are you, Matt?'

Matt laughed. 'It might come to that, Jack.'

Jack looked at him earnestly now. 'Are you saying what I think you're saying, Matt?'

Matt nodded, the pride showing in his eyes. 'Aye, Jack. Dolly's expecting. She's been to t'doctor, he's confirmed it, she's a good two months on, and she's fine.'

Jack slapped him on the back and said, 'That's just the sort of news we could do with, Matt. After months of gloom and farewells galore on this farm, we're due some good news and new arrivals. Well done, and congratulations.'

The two men discussed the merits of larger families and Matt was clearly very proud of Dolly, although, when he returned to tend his flock after the break, he did have memories of his twins, the first little Sam and his sister, Sally, both killed in a traffic accident following the death of their mother, Peggy. Peggy had been Jack's sister . . .

But Matt was enough of a realist to know that life must continue and it was the future that mattered now, not the past. He left Jack to continue work.

'Quality not quantity!' shouted Jack from the distance, the wind carrying his voice across the dale to a happy Matt.

As the news from Emmerdale became distinctly happier, Mrs Bates's marriage had come to its sad end. She had said farewell to her husband, Malcolm, in agreeing to a divorce so that he could marry Sonia. By the terms of the divorce settlement, she would receive an allowance and help with Nick's school fees. There'd be assistance, too, for Kathy if she went to college.

The house in Hotten would be sold, and so Mrs Bates would have a small capital sum to her name, not enough to form an income but sufficient to create a little nest egg for her own future and perhaps the occasional holiday. But the house that Turner had allocated her in Beckindale was her salvation; Seth and the other estate workers had made a wonderful job of decorating it and bringing it up to standard, sometimes aided by Seth's donkey which occasionally popped in, especially when Alan Turner arrived to supervise the work. Somehow, it knew when Turner was walking through Beckindale and followed him like a dog.

In the late summer of that year, Caroline Bates moved into the cottage and started her new life in Beckindale. At first, this did not suit her children, both of whom were accustomed to living in a busy Yorkshire town with entertainment, sports and leisure amenities. Instead, they found themselves in Beckindale during the summer months when the most exciting events were the annual cricket match between NY and the village eleven, and the annual WI street fair and church garden party. She knew it would be difficult keeping them cheerful and occupied in these circumstances, but she would certainly try.

Chapter Ten

The long days of summer passed and a successful
haytime cleared the fields of the standing grass and
filled the air with the sweetness of new-mown hay.
Jackie showed a remarkable determination to make
a total recovery from his injuries. He was working
hard at becoming mobile again, getting his wasted
muscles back to work and training his mind to accept
his present limitations. In the hospital, he was allocated his own pair of crutches and shown how to
walk with them, how to balance and how to manoeuvre himself up and down steps, through doors
and into confined spaces. He fell once or twice and
bruised himself from time to time, but it was not
long before he could make rapid progress from one
end of the ward to the other. The good news was
that his fractured pelvis had responded to the treatment; the chromium pins had enabled the bones to
knit together and they would become just as strong
as they had been before the accident. His internal
injuries were healing too and his lungs were no
longer causing concern.

It was at this time that Jack Sugden received a call
from the hospital; it was Jackie's consultant, Mr
Smale, asking if Jack or Pat would call to see him
within the next day or two to discuss the possibility
of Jackie's return home in the fairly near future.
Jack said he would be only too pleased. Pat and

168

Annie were delighted at the prospect and on the day of Jack's visit, declined his offer to a lift into Hotten; they said they would stay at home and begin the preparations for Jackie's return.

Jack did say there was no immediate rush because no date had been suggested, but this did not deter Pat and Annie. Pat rushed out to tell Tom, who was working in the mistle.

On the following Wednesday morning, Jack drove into Hotten to complete one or two chores before visiting the hospital. There was a minor bank trans-action to complete concerning a renewal and upgrad-ing of the insurance for the farm equipment, a haircut to organise, some spares to buy for the ailing tractor, some baler twine and a tub of grease to purchase and sundry other jobs which had been awaiting such a trip. Even though his appointment with Mr Smale was not until eleven-thirty, Jack left Emmerdale shortly after nine, taking Sandie with him. She was enjoying a later start today, for she was helping out at a house sale this evening and he said he could complete his business before meeting Smale.

'Bye,' he said. 'Let's hope I bring good news back home.'

Pat watched him leave, having kissed him good-bye, and she stood at the door of the farm kitchen, wistfully watching his Land Rover until it was out of sight. Annie approached her.

'You'll have to learn to trust him sometime, luv,' she said, with a full understanding of Pat's internal agony.

'It's the first time for ages he's gone like that, just

like he used to when he was seeing Karen. Taking Sandie to Hotten and leaving early so he could have more time with her.'

'I trust him,' Annie said. 'All he wants now is you and Jackie; I know that, Pat.'

'And all I want is Jackie home again, in full health, and a husband who is mine and mine alone,' and there was worry in Pat's voice.

'Happen today will make those wishes come true.' Annie smiled at her daughter-in-law. 'Now, come on, if Jackie is coming home, we've a room to get ready.'

They decided that if Jackie was still using crutches when he returned, he'd have to use the parlour as a bedroom. That would mean fetching a bed and even a wardrobe downstairs, though they'd need some help for that. It was going to be a busy morning.

Jack too had a busy morning in Hotten and managed to finish all his business calls before visiting Mr Smale at the hospital; he even got his hair cut. He was shown into Smale's cramped office before seeing Jackie.

'Well, Mr Sugden, I suppose this is the news you and your family have been waiting for.'

'If you're going to tell me he's coming home soon, then yes, it is.'

'The lad's made very good progress, Mr Sugden. When he came in here, I must admit I was very concerned about him, about his internal injuries more than the obvious pelvic fracture, but he's mended nicely. Now, the reason I called you here is to say that we are almost ready to release him, and I wanted you and your family to be well prepared.'

Smale went on to outline the problems of having an invalid at home for a long time. At first, Jackie would be on crutches, which in themselves were always awkward to manoeuvre on steps, uneven ground and certainly in farmyards! After a period on underarm crutches, he would graduate to elbow crutches, lightweight ones which would assist his legs to return to their full strength, and finally, after several more weeks, he would be able to make do with a simple walking stick before eventually casting that aside. But Jackie's pelvis was still weak and liable to damage if he was careless, and his leg muscles had not yet returned to their full strength, but there would be regular checks at the hospital, with Jackie having to visit Hotten once a week initially, then once a fortnight and finally once a month until his recovery was complete.

'What I'm saying, Mr Sugden,' Smale went on, 'is that a heavy responsibility does fall upon you and your family. Our policy is to return our patients to their homes only if we feel the family is able to cope. It is a burden, make no mistake about it. Jackie is going to try and rush things, he'll want to go out with his pals, to walk around the farm, to do all the things he did before the accident, and he's going to tire very easily. Worse still, he will get very upset when he finds he just cannot do what he wants. There could be bouts of depression and anger. Even so, it is our belief that final recuperation is much better in a family atmosphere.

'Now,' Smale concluded, 'having explained some of the main problems, do you feel you can cope with him at home?'

171

Jack said he had no doubt at all. He told Smale about the downstairs parlour which could be converted into a bedroom and persuaded the specialist that Jackie would be well cared for.

'So,' Jack continued. 'When are we talking about? How soon is he coming home?'

'We can't give you a precise date yet, Mr Sugden, as we've a few more tests to complete and checks to make. But I'm confident it will be within the month, maybe even within the fortnight.'

Jack's face expressed his sheer delight and he knew that the whole family would make Jackie's recovery a happy time.

'Good, then I can put our procedures in motion,' smiled Mr Smale. 'Now, would you like to tell him the good news?'

Mr Smale led Jack through to the ward where Jackie was practising on his crutches. For a moment, he had no idea Jack was there, and he was demonstrating to Stephen just how clever he was at turning a full circle on one heel just by using one crutch. Jack watched him with pride and then applauded and shouted, 'Bravo! And what's your next trick?'

Jackie flopped onto his bed at the sound of Jack's voice and said, 'Oh, hi, Jack. It's not visiting time, is it?'

'No,' Jack laughed. 'But I was in Hotten with nowt special to do, so I thought I'd come and see you!'

'Ha, ha!' Jackie pretended to laugh at Jack's cheap joke. 'Anyway, it's good to see you. What did you think of my pirouette, then?'

'Stick a rake in one hand as you do that, and you'd

172

soon clean up the hay in our stack yard!' laughed Jack.

'I wouldn't mind doing that, Jack.' Jackie was serious now. 'I'd give anything to be out of here, raking up the hay and clipping the sheep. I was thinking, when I get out of here, I might try a flock of my own, you know, a small number to begin with, and then build it up and mebbe show them at the Great Yorkshire Show or the North Yorkshire Show or somewhere.'

'Well, that's why I'm here,' Jack smiled. 'Mr Smale has been telling me how well you're doing and he reckons, if you behave yourself, you could be out of here soon. Within a month – mebbe even less.'

'You're joking? I don't believe it!' Jackie looked at his crutches, at his plastered leg, and suddenly, he felt nervous about the idea.

'But, I mean, they wouldn't let me out like this . . .'

'We feel we can let you home soon, Jackie,' said Smale. 'You'll have to come back in for the plaster to be removed, of course, and for other treatments, but we feel your pelvis has knitted now, and that there is no reason why you should not continue your recovery at home.'

Jackie stood up and performed another of his twirls on the crutches and shouted with delight, 'Hey, Steve, hear that? They're letting me out of here . . .'

Jack remained for another half an hour and they discussed the problems that would have to be overcome, but Jackie found it difficult to conceal his

173

delight. Jack left the hospital in a buoyant mood and, as it was lunch time, he decided to treat himself to a bar snack at one of the town centre inns. He drove back into the town and parked near the post office. Just across the street was a florist's shop. On impulse, he went in and bought a dozen dark red roses and a small card upon which he wrote a message of love to Pat. Then he went out.

And as he left the shop, he bumped into Karen Moore.

'Karen!' The happiness was clear in his voice. 'Hi. How are you?'

'All right,' she said. 'You?'

'I've just been to the hospital,' he said after a moment of awkwardness. 'Jackie's coming out soon . . . as you probably know, he got knocked down by a car . . . Er, look,' he continued, 'I'm going to have lunch next, at a pub, I thought. A bar snack. Do you want to come and join me? No strings attached – just a friendly lunch for old time's sake?'

She looked into his eyes, her own moist at the happy memories of their times together, but she shook her head.

'No, Jack. I don't think so. Not now. I'd love to, you know that, but . . .'

'I know,' he said. And without another word, he eased one of the red roses from the bouquet and gave it to her. She looked at it and then came forward and kissed him on the cheek.

'Thanks, Jack. Bye.'

'Bye, Karen,' and he watched her walk away, his heart aching as he knew that he still loved her – just as he also loved Pat. He looked at the roses, sighed with a massive heave of his shoulders, and went to his car to place them inside. Then he went for lunch.

After lunch, he bought a box of chocolates for his mother, then drove straight home. He kissed Pat as he handed her the roses, and pecked Ma on the cheek too, before relating his news about Jackie. They were all thrilled and showed Jack the parlour which they had prepared.

'We've moved a lot of stuff out, but you'll have to help us carry a bed and wardrobe downstairs,' Pat said. 'We thought we'd use those out of Grandad's room.'

'Fine, sure. He'll like this, he said he wanted to use the parlour and asked me to make sure his record player was there. It's at Demdyke just now.' And so the family prepared for Jackie's return.

Pat placed her red roses in a large vase on the mantelpiece and it was over a cup of tea later that afternoon that she said, 'Jack, those roses. They are lovely, really.'

'They're for a lovely woman!' he kissed her.

'Thanks,' and she felt happier now than she had for many months. 'There's only eleven, though, they usually come in dozens, don't they?'

'I knocked the head off one when I was putting them in the car,' he lied easily.

'Trust you,' she chuckled.

'Look luv,' he said suddenly. 'I was thinking – ages ago, I said you and I should get away for a weekend but we've been too busy, so, well, how about this weekend? Before Jackie comes home, I mean. I'm sure Ma and the rest of them will cope.'

'Oh, Jack, I would really like that. Where shall we go?'

'Not far, I don't want to spend the weekend travelling. I know a place that means summat to you and me . . . a surprise. So shall we do it?'

'Oh. yes, please,' she smiled.

Jack and Pat went to Knaresborough, where they had met and fallen in love so many years ago, a place where their liaison had led to Jackie's birth.

For this romantic weekend, they stayed in a beautiful old inn and explored the town again, visiting its fascinating old castle high above the gorge, boating on the River Nidd, seeing the petrifying well which turned ordinary objects into stone, and exploring Mother Shipton's cave with its echoes of her curious prophesies.

Back at the farm in the days before Jackie returned, Tom Merrick, who had worked so well alongside Matt and Jack, said he had to leave for Aberdeen because he'd been offered a new job. He went to say his farewells to Jackie, kissed Pat a fond goodbye, and thanked Jack for being a tower of strength to Jackie. They all agreed Tom had changed, mellowed perhaps, and they knew they would miss him, Sandie especially.

Sandie also lost a companion in Mike West because, in his quest for work, he had found a job at an hotel in Skegness. He decided he would take it; he realised there was no future for him in Beckindale, and although this job was only a seasonal one in the kitchens, it did offer some prospects of finding further work in hotels. He said farewell to

Sandie as a friend; he had long ago accepted Sandie could never love him.

By this time, Beckindale had become accustomed to the sight of Amos in his beekeeping outfit and to Seth's donkey which had eaten everything it could reach. It had been banished from his allotment because it had eaten everyone's flowers, having shown a remarkable ability to escape from wherever it was confined.

It continued to shadow Alan Turner wherever possible and also retained its love for Amos's bees. In time a solution was reached when Seth thought that Jessie would be ideal for trimming the grave-yard, and, with the consent of the Reverend Donald Hinton, Jessie was accommodated at the vicarage. But she would not stay there. Her dexterity in opening the gate enabled her to return to the bees. Finally it was agreed that, to encourage Jessie to remain in the graveyard, Amos should reposition his bees there. And so this came to pass. Bees and donkey living happily together among the tomb-stones, although the donkey always kept an eye upon the village street in case Alan Turner should stroll past.

The efforts of Seth and Amos to beat one another in the election for presidency of the Beckindale Allotments and Horticultural Society came to noth-ing because a rank outsider was elected – Walter, the silent man who drank each night and each lunchtime in the Woolpack. He was voted in because he never disagreed with anyone and no one could anticipate his actions upon any matter.

Dolly continued her barmaid's job at the Woolpack during those weeks, enjoying the extra cash
which she was putting aside. She and Matt had
decided to have a break before their new baby
arrived and Matt, in a uncharacteristic move, had
booked a late summer holiday in Spain. This had
encouraged Dolly to work even longer hours at the
pub, which in turn pleased Amos because of the
extra customers she attracted. One of her ideas was
to sell Woolpack teeshirts and she proved an ideal
model by wearing one of them herself, an act which
sent temperatures rising among the male customers.
And Amos remained convinced that the new boom
in business was due to the quality of his ale . . .

When the time came for Jackie's homecoming, he
was asked to ring his family himself. With his new
friend Nurse Sita Sharma to encourage him, he set
off upon his crutches, using skills taught him by the
physiotherapist (whom he called a physio-terrorist)
and eventually arrived at the telephone. It had been
a difficult journey for he'd had to negotiate trolleys
in the corridors, two flights of stairs and now he had
to squeeze into the tight corner which contained the
telephone. And then, as he picked up the instrument
to call Emmerdale, he realised he had forgotten to
bring any money. He couldn't reverse the charges
because that phone would not accept incoming calls
so Nurse Sharma had to run back and find some.

It was Pat who answered. 'Hello, Emmerdale
Farm, Pat Sugden.'

'Mum? It's me, Jackie. They've given me a date
for coming home. Isn't that smashing?'

'Oh, luv, I am pleased. When?'

'Friday. I'm leaving at eleven.'

'Me and Jack'll come and meet you, you'll need some clothes.'

'No, no need, Mum. They're taking me in the ambulance, my leg'll never get into a car, it's still rigid with all that plaster. So I'll be there about dinner time, eh? I'm ready for some of Ma's Yorkshire puddings and onion gravy.'

'We'll come anyway, to see you . . .'

'Well, you don't have to. I'll be in pyjamas because I'm still confined to bed, although they do let me practise walking and sitting.'

'We are looking forward to you coming home, Jackie,' she said gently. 'We've fixed the parlour up for you . . .'

'Not Demdyke, then?'

'Course not, you need somebody to look after you.'

'I might bring my own nurse!' he laughed. 'Sita's her name, her dad's a doctor in Hotten.'

'These hospital romances aren't the same when you're home, Jackie,' she cautioned him.

'This one will be,' he said. 'Anyroad, mum, see you on Friday. Tell Annie to have the Yorkshire puddings in the oven!'

Chapter Eleven

Jackie found life back at Emmerdale far from easy. He did enjoy sleeping in the parlour, but found that his movements were so restricted. His world was limited to the kitchen and the parlour for he'd discovered that the steps outside the farm and the uneven surface of the yard made walking very difficult. For a time, he found himself more hemmed in than he'd been at the hospital with its long corridors and numerous patients to talk to. He did make lots of phone calls to Sita and then he wondered if she would visit him here at the farm. He made the suggestion during one of his telephone calls and to his surprise and pleasure, she agreed to come to tea one Sunday afternoon when her duties permitted.

It was at this point that Annie tackled him about his untidiness. She castigated him about leaving his records and tapes in a dreadful mess, leaving newspapers and magazines lying around, and not bothering to empty the ashtrays after visits by his friends. There were even empty beer cans under the bed.

'Look, Jackie, just because you're ill doesn't mean you shouldn't do a little for yourself now and again.'

'It's so boring, Annie, just shut up in here and the kitchen.'

'But if you want Sita to come, you'll have to make sure your room's fit for her to visit. Remember she's a nurse and nurses like to see tidiness.'

He did make an attempt to tidy the mess and Sita's forthcoming visit lifted his spirits. It would be the first time she had seen Jackie outside the hospital and in his view, it showed that she was fond of him in a way that was more than just a nurse-patient relationship. She called to say she would arrive in Beckindale on the 3.45pm bus from Hotten on Sunday and Jackie said he'd be at the bus stop to meet her. With this incentive, he renewed his efforts to walk around the farm, at first having immense difficulty negotiating the more tricky areas of the buildings, but by hard work and practice, he was able to enter the mistle and the barns.

With care, he was able to hobble into the field behind the house and this gave him the impression he might be able to take a stroll around the village. On the day of Sita's arrival, he said he would travel in the Land Rover to meet her – if Jack would take him down to the bus stop near the Woolpack to await Sita. Jack said he would wait and drive them home, but Jackie said he wanted to show Sita around the village, and the churchyard with the family graves. He was sure he could cope with that short walk.

'If I get into trouble, I can always ring the farm and ask for a car to come for us,' he said.

Jack smiled. 'Aye, right. Do that. I won't be far away.'

When Sita arrived, she found Jackie sitting at one of the tables on the Woolpack's forecourt, beaming with happiness. They kissed briefly, and she said, 'You've walked to meet me?'

'I cannot tell a lie,' he grinned. 'Jack brought me

down, but I thought I'd show you the village before we go to the house for tea.'

'I'd like that.' She looked at the crutches. 'It'll get me used to the area before I meet your folks.'

'You met 'em in hospital,' he laughed.

'It's different when you go to a person's home,' she replied. 'Hospital is all part of my job, this time I'm on show as myself, as your friend . . .'

'I like showing you off!' he grinned. 'Come on, let's see how I cope among the tombstones!'

They enjoyed the walk, with Jackie explaining how the little church had seen many of the weddings, funerals and baptisms of the Sugden family over several generations. Sita pointed out that she was not a Christian and therefore would not marry in this kind of building, though Jackie seemed not to hear her words nor to comprehend them fully as he steered her through his ancestors. Eventually the physical effort became too much for him. He had to rest from time to time, and finally popped into the kiosk to ring Jack for transport to Emmerdale.

Annie and Pat prepared a fine farmhouse tea for their guest and made Sita most welcome. She entertained them with tales of Jackie's antics in hospital, and told them of her father's work as a doctor in Hotten. He was in the same practice as Dr Perry who sometimes visited patients in Beckindale and Sita explained how she looked after her father, being his only child, because her mother had died several years ago. Annie, Pat, Jack and Sandie thought her a delightful girl and they all felt glad that Jackie had found himself another lovely girlfriend.

Sita remained for some time after tea, with Annie

showing her the poultry and geese, and Pat taking
her around the cows during their second milking
session and up to see the sheep and their growing
lambs in the fields. Sita said she had enjoyed her
visit and felt that Jackie had improved since leaving
hospital. She felt he would soon be managing without his crutches and asked Pat to give him every
encouragement to try – but he might need his
confidence bolstering before attempting that next
stage of his recovery. Pat and Sita returned to the
house, with Sita saying she must catch the 7.30 bus
back to Hotten. Pat said there was just time for a
cup of tea and another bite to eat.

But as Sita was settling down with Jackie at her
side, Matt rushed into the kitchen, red-faced and
clearly upset. He sought Annie.

'Ma, quick,' he said. 'It's Dolly. She's bleeding
. . . she thought she'd got cramp, but . . .'

'She's pregnant?' Sita was on her feet in a
moment.

'Yes,' said Matt, recognising Sita from Jackie's
frequent descriptions of her.

'I'll come.' Sita acted swiftly and followed Matt
over to the cottage where Dolly was on the settee,
pale and sick with worry. Sita made a swift but
skilled examination as she questioned Dolly, and
then said, 'Can you get her into bed, Mr Skilbeck?
Help her upstairs – I will ring my father, he's the
duty doctor this evening.'

'What is it?' Matt's agony showed on his face now.
'I mean, she's not going to lose it, is she? Not after
all this time, not after we'd planned . . .'

183

'I don't know,' Sita said firmly but with compassion. 'But you must get her into bed, gently. I'll help.'

Sita rang for her father and gave him explicit directions to Emmerdale, and then she and Matt helped Dolly up to the bedroom where they laid her on the bed. Sita told Dolly to lie very still and to take deep breaths as she tried to relax. Relaxation was vital just now. Matt remained at her bedside, holding her hand. Little Sam was fast asleep in the next room.

Dr Sharma arrived within half-an-hour and asked Matt to leave him and Sita with Dolly. He was a tall, distinguished man, obviously proud of his Indian origins.

They were with her for about three-quarters of an hour, with Matt pacing up and down the room below. And then he heard heavy footsteps on the stairs and Dr Sharma came into the kitchen.

'I'm sorry,' he said to Matt. 'There was nothing we could do. Nothing.'

'How is she?' he asked.

'She's sleeping now. Sita is seeing to the bed, she's adept at changing sheets in these circumstances. I've given your wife a sedative, Mr Skilbeck, so she will rest and sleep all night. She will be fine physically but she will need a lot of care and love from you.'

'What caused it?' asked Matt.

Sharma thought for a moment. 'I cannot say because I do not know. Anything could have caused it – but there may not even be a reason, Mr Skilbeck. Nature can be cruel at times.'

'Aye,' said Matt bitterly. 'It can.'

Chapter Twelve

Jackie's recovery was greatly helped by Sita's visits. It was her efforts that encouraged him to be more adventurous in his disability. She made him walk around the farm; she made him try without his heavy crutches, convinced him it was time to sample elbow crutches, then prompted him just to use a walking stick. That Jackie loved Sita was never in doubt and this helped enormously in persuading him to visit the hospital for his regular checks and physiotherapy treatment. Everyone hoped Jackie would not become too dependent upon her, either in his emotional life or in his physical recuperation.

Getting to know Sita had been one pleasant outcome of Jackie's accident. The major bonus, of course, had been its role in the reconciliation between Jack and Pat. It had united them as a family with Jackie as the focal point and it had brought pride and joy once more to the whole family at Emmerdale.

Jack was acutely aware of the problems and turmoil he had caused the farm and the family, and he accepted his guilt. His immense sorrow at hurting Pat had deepened his love both for her and for Jackie, and he fully recognised the invaluable part his natural son had played in cementing his relationships. They were now a true family.

Jack did his best to befriend Matt as he and Dolly

recovered from the loss of their unborn child and he spent lots of time with Jackie too, laughing with him, coaxing him into regular exercise and fuelling him with the determination necessary to lead a full and busy life. Jackie responded and Jack realised that a magnificent new relationship was developing. It was such a direct contrast to their past antagonism and helped Jack to come to terms with his family responsibilities. But as he busied himself around the farm, sometimes lost in his own thoughts, Jack did not notice the change in Pat's behaviour. In recent weeks, she had become somewhat secretive, quiet and even withdrawn. It was Sandie who first noticed these changes.

One occasion was during a shopping trip to Hotten. Annie, Pat and Sandie had all gone into town, each intent on having an enjoyable day out with lunch and a bout of shopping. Sandie had told them they could leave the car in one of the office's parking spaces at Hotten Mart because it would be free, being a Saturday. They were using Annie's car; Pat was the driver, with Annie in the front passenger seat as Sandie guided her into the right place.

They climbed out, arming themselves with shopping bags and handbags, and then Karen emerged from the office. She hadn't recognised the car, and had been about to chase it away from the private parking area, when she saw Sandie. But it was Pat who spotted Karen first and waved cheerily at her, calling, 'Hi, Karen, thanks for the parking space.' Sandie and Karen looked quite taken aback at her friendliness.

They'd had a successful trip, each buying some

clothes and shoes. When they drove off to find some lunch, Sandie noticed further odd behaviour from her mother. Pat almost drove straight out of a junction, causing a lorry to brake violently, but instead of displaying shock and annoyance she had waved cheerily at the angry driver. Then at lunch she left a five-pound tip for the waiter. Normally she left either a pound or perhaps two if she was feeling particularly generous.

'You're in a funny mood, Mum,' Sandie had said as they drove home.

'Am I?' Pat had smiled at her daughter. 'I'm happy, that's all. Just happy.'

The others began to notice Pat's changing attitudes, too. The following Monday, she drove into Hotten alone, saying she wanted to change a dress she'd bought because it was too tight, but she spent a long time in town and came home looking as if she had won a fortune. When she came into the kitchen, Annie saw she was singing to herself and beaming all over.

'Hello, luv,' Annie welcomed her. 'You're looking happy. Had a good day?'

'Yes, I got that dress changed. And yes, ma, I think I've had a very good day.' Then she asked, 'Er, is Jack around?'

'He's feeding the calves, he shouldn't be long,' Annie said. 'He's due in for a cup of tea and a scone any time now.'

'Tell him I'm home when he comes in,' she smiled. 'I'll be in our room, trying my new dress on.'

'All right, luv,' answered Annie, puzzling after Pat as she vanished upstairs humming to herself.

When Jack came in to wash his hands, Annie said, 'Pat's back, Jack. She says to tell you she's in your room. She's in a funny mood, Jack, summat's got into her.'

He laughed. 'Has she been spending on new clothes?'

'She did change a dress she got on Saturday, said it was too tight.'

'She'll want my expert opinion on her new look,' he grinned. 'OK, I'll go up. Won't be long.'

When he entered their room, Pat was wearing the new dress and standing before the mirror, smoothing it over her figure and trying to determine if it was a good fit and whether it suited her. She twirled before the mirror, sending the skirts billowing out as he whistled in his appreciation.

'Nice,' he said, taking her in his arms and kissing her. 'You look good – that shade of green suits you, it makes your hair look great . . . yeh, I like it, luv.'

'You don't think it's too tight?' She stood away from him and ran her hands across her stomach and down her hips.

'Well, I didn't like to say,' he smiled, 'but I did think you'd put on a bit of weight lately. Ma said you'd changed this dress because the other was too tight, so mebbe you have put on a bit. But this 'un's not too tight, you look great in it, you really do.'

She took his hand and led him to the bed, making his sit down beside her.

'Jack,' she said. 'Jack, darling. I've been to the doctor today, in Hotten . . .'

'Doctor?' he puzzled. 'Summat wrong?'

'No,' she beamed at him. 'Everything's right, oh, it's all so very right, Jack.'

He said nothing now and simply gazed at her in some bewilderment.

'Jack,' she said. 'I'm pregnant. I didn't know how to tell you . . . but . . . well, here I am, telling you.'

'I don't believe it!' he cried, flinging his arms about her. 'Are you sure? Absolutely sure?'

She nodded, the tears of happiness running down her cheeks as Jack kissed her over and over again. They remained in their room for a long time, happier together than they had been for a long, long time.

'How are we going to tell the others? Ma? Sandie? Jackie?' Pat smiled as she wiped her eyes. 'I can see them now, saying we're too old, we're old enough to know better . . .'

'It doesn't matter what anybody else thinks, luv,' he said. 'It's our baby, yours and mine . . .'

And they hugged each other all over again. Then Jack said, 'Come on, there's a cuppa downstairs. Ma's waiting. Shall we tell her now?'

'Yes, you tell her, Jack. I'd like you to do that.'

They left their room and as they reached the door, Jack turned to her and said, 'Pat, luv. Who's going to tell Dolly?'

Fontana Paperbacks: Fiction

Fontana is a leading paperback publisher of fiction.
Below are some recent titles.

- ☐ THE HEATH Abigail Frith £3.95
- ☐ PATRIOT GAMES Tom Clancy £3.95
- ☐ YES MAMA Helen Forrester £3.50
- ☐ SKIN DEEP Helene Mansfield £3.50
- ☐ HEAVEN AND HELL John Jakes £4.95
- ☐ THE NOONDAY DEVIL Alan Judd £2.95
- ☐ SHORT OF GLORY Alan Judd £3.95
- ☐ A SEMI-DETACHED WOMAN Polly Graham £3.50
- ☐ THE SECOND MIDNIGHT Andrew Taylor £3.95
- ☐ REINDEER MOON Elizabeth M. Thomas £3.95
- ☐ THE WELL OF TIME Tom Henighan £3.95

You can buy Fontana paperbacks at your local bookshop or
newsagent. Or you can order them from Fontana Paperbacks,
Cash Sales Department, Box 29, Douglas, Isle of Man. Please
send a cheque, postal or money order (not currency) worth the
purchase price plus 22p per book for postage (maximum postage
required is £3.00 for orders within the UK).

NAME (Block letters) _____

ADDRESS _____

_____

While every effort is made to keep prices low, it is sometimes necessary to increase them at short
notice. Fontana Paperbacks reserve the right to show new retail prices on covers which may differ
from those previously advertised in the text or elsewhere.